SIREN SILENCE

The Fate of Cpt. Bacchus:
A King of the Caves Novella

Brandon M Wilborn

Beacon Creative Publishing LLC

MERIDIAN, IDAHO

Beacon Creative Publishing LLC
1740 E Fairview Ave #82
Meridian, ID 83642

Publisher's Note: This is a work of fiction. Names, characters, places, and incidents are a product of the author's imagination. Locales and public names are sometimes used for atmospheric purposes. Any resemblance to actual people, living or dead, or to businesses, companies, events, institutions, or locales is completely coincidental. All uses of The Holy Bible in the main text are paraphrases with modification prepared from the author's own translation. The New International Version was used only for the epigraph.

Book Layout © 2017 BookDesignTemplates.com
Cover art & design by Darko Tomic **paganus.weebly.com/**
Map by Veronika Wunderer **www.veronika-wunderer.com**

Book Title/ Author Name. -- 1st ed.
ISBN 978-1-7337922-3-3 Paperback
ISBN 978-1-7337922-2-6 eBook

To those who hear the Siren's call

"The night is nearly over; the day is almost here. So let us put aside the deeds of darkness and put on the armor of light."

–ROMANS 13:12 (NIV)

Contents

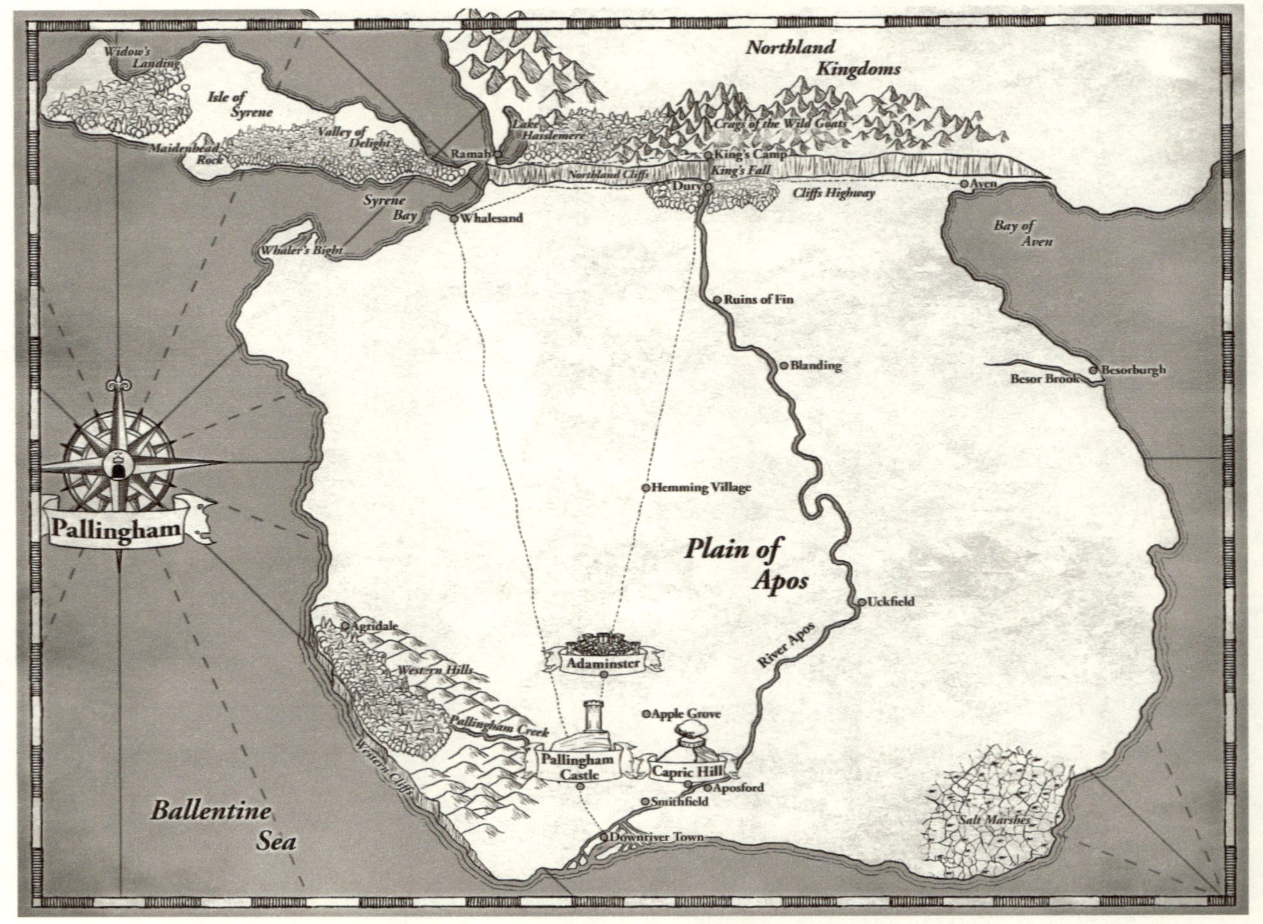

Widow's Landing
Isle of Syrene
Valley of Delight
Maidenhead Rock
Lake Hasslemere
Ramah
Northland Cliffs
Syrene Bay
Whaler's Bight
Whalesand
Northland Kingdoms
Crags of the Wild Goats
King's Camp
King's Fall
Dury
Cliffs Highway
Aven
Bay of Aven
Ruins of Fin
Blanding
Besor Brook
Besorburgh
Pallingham
Hemming Village
Plain of Apos
Uckfield
River Apos
Agridale
Adaminster
Western Hills
Apple Grove
Pallingham Creek
Pallingham Castle
Capric Hill
Aposford
Smithfield
Western Cliffs
Downriver Town
Salt Marshes
Ballentine Sea

Ashore

Captain Dylan Bacchus dragged himself onto the beach as the tide tugged him back into the bay. The music that had enticed him to leave his ship for the island filled his head, driving him through frigid waves. His body shook. His breath came in trembling jolts.

The siren song took away his sense like a night of heavy drinking. He tried to stand but only felt his face digging into the wet sand when he fell. Rising on his knees, he sputtered and crunched grit between his teeth. Faces peeked through the trees ahead—beautiful faces, with the enchanting voices that had called him here. They had been dancing on the shore when he jumped in the water. The most beautiful women he had ever seen were dancing naked on the beach, inviting him to join them with their song. Why were they hiding now?

Another sound was coming from his right. It was loud and clashed with the singing of the beautiful faces. He looked around. A man ran at him, yelling. He held something. A sense inside Captain Bacchus muted the singing beauties in time for him to roll on his side and kick at his attacker.

Pain shot up Bacchus' leg, into his body. The thing the man was holding was a dagger, now protruding from Bacchus' remaining boot, midway up his left calf.

The attacker was on top of him. They rolled in the sand and Bacchus felt wild fists pounding on his head. Instinct took over. He grabbed his own blade from his belt and jabbed it into the man's right side again and again until the blows stopped.

They rolled again. He was now atop the other man. In a moment, he saw the peppered beard and thinning hair, the dark brown eyes wide with surprise. He knew this man.

"Captain!" the sailor coughed out, spattering blood on Bacchus' face.

It was one of his crew.

Before he remembered the name, the Song returned. Only one thing mattered—the beautiful ones.

Bacchus left his blade in the body and crawled higher up the beach as they emerged from the trees. Indeed, they had the most beautiful faces he had ever seen, each more exotic and appealing than the last. Their bodies were slender, but shapely in all the ways he liked. He tried standing, but his strength failed him as they approached. He fell forward. Then he noticed their feet.

Below the knees, each one had feet with gnarled, gray skin, and cruel, sharp talons. They were bird feet, hunter's feet, like those of the osprey after which he had named his ship. Even their song could not stop his revulsion.

The sirens ignored him while they collected the other corpses that washed ashore. Then the two most beautiful ones grabbed his shoulders and dragged him off the beach, into the forest.

Vision

Kurian Abramson woke with the haunting music of the sirens still lingering in his mind. His brow was sweaty, even though the air was cold and showed his breath. His previous brush with the creatures was bad enough to create his dreams, but this felt like something different. It had a feel of reality unlike any dream he'd ever had.

He dropped his feet to the floor and sat on the edge of the bed—his father's bed. They had shared the room when he was a child. His father had passed into sleep forever in that same bed only days before, and Kurian's old sleeping mat was too small for him now.

A rooster crowed, and Kurian rose and opened the shutters. Stars still filled the sky above while the Eastern horizon held a touch of sapphire light.

He still wasn't used to being able to see the stars. Would he ever be? The land of Pallingham had been covered with clouds and mist for generations, until the day he met the King of the Caves, and all the prophecies about the treasure Kurian had been training to protect came true. The clouds cleared and the sun blazed with the dawn. The river Apos flowed again, and a new king was named—Kurian himself. His father had died then, the only tragedy in a day of victory. None of it felt real yet. He didn't feel like a king, especially sitting in his poor childhood home.

The stars and the early light of daybreak soothed him, and a cool breeze through the window made him shiver. He had trouble shaking the dream that had woken him. Those bird feet.

A few minutes later, Kurian had dressed and walked quietly but purposefully through the small town he had renamed Viviford. Three men challenged him as he approached the bridge, then let him pass when they saw his face in the torchlight.

"Early morning, young Kurian," said a man from his childhood. He couldn't remember the name.

An older man slapped the first's head. "Show some respect," he said. "That's our new king." All three saluted.

Kurian smiled and nodded. "Little need for formalities, gentlemen. We don't have a kingdom yet."

Once over the bridge, Kurian passed quickly through the overturned turf of the recent battlefield where they had defeated the army of Lord Evasius, the man who had razed his monastery home and pursued him and his friends on their entire journey to find the King of the Caves. The smell of smoke drifted up from the southern edge where they had burned the dead locust creatures that Evasius' witches had called up from the ground. He was glad he didn't have to see the remaining carnage on his way to the foot of Capric hill. Ravens combed the battlefield after the larger scavengers had given up. One of them cried out loudly and took flight as Kurian arrived at the crumbled and charred gates of the Capric order.

The dream that had woken him felt urgent, a call to complete things undone. It compelled him to do the one thing he knew he had neglected in the days since the battle.

His legs seemed to work from memory as they drove him up the steep side of the hill, just as they had ten thousand times when he was a student here. It felt like a lifetime ago, but less than a month before, he had eaten, slept, studied, and trained in the same buildings that were now charred husks around him.

Dawn broke as he crested the hill. The few stone structures on the summit were black and roofless. The sacred Oak was burned and broken, its remaining trunk like a diseased finger pointing its accusations at heaven. Kurian's breath caught in his throat, and he sobbed at the complete destruction. He didn't care about the order or the monastery. But he wept for the men slaughtered here, good men whom he had called brothers.

He fell on his knees to pray.

A few moments later Kurian heard steps behind him. "I'm glad you finally came," said a voice husky with emotion.

"I'm glad it's you, Tobin," Kurian said. He wiped his eyes and stood up. It soothed him to see a shy grin from his best friend.

"Your old neighbors told me you were here," Tobin said. "You've been so busy organizing the village to clean up the horrible mess down there and dealing with all the soldiers who said they want to change sides, I wasn't sure you'd have time for this place. I took the liberty of raising volunteers and gathering up the bodies to prepare our brothers for burial."

"Thank you," Kurian whispered.

Tobin closed his eyes. "I...wasn't able to recognize any of them." There were no tears. Kurian knew Tobin had already spent them all.

"I thought about burying them," Tobin said, "like we would have before. But I wasn't sure. That would have been the order's way, and things are so very different now. We're beyond the simplicity of the Rule."

Kurian looked toward the Oak. Nearby, a set of stone steps led down, into the hill. "They died for God and their brothers. We'll honor them by burying them with their brothers in the tombs," he said. "Arrange a memorial in the square. Only those who knew them."

"That will be good," Tobin nodded and turned to leave.

Kurian watched a raven circle above and sighed.

"Please be quick," he said. "There's something else we have to do."

Tobin stopped and waited. He was unusually quiet.

"Three nights now, I've had the same dream," Kurian started, then lowered his head, struggling to explain. "But it's not a dream, it's more like a..."

"Vision?" Tobin asked.

"Exactly! It's as real as the vision I had in the caves, with the King, but horrible." Kurian looked up and saw the steely blue gaze and slightly raised brow Tobin always had when he knew the answer. "You've had one, too," he said.

Tobin nodded once. "The song." Then he shuddered.

"I don't know how," said Kurian, "but Captain Bacchus is alive. I believe we're meant to rescue him."

Delirious

Captain Bacchus heard footsteps nearby—crunching leaves followed by rustling in the sand. He opened his eyes to a blurry scene. Light was everywhere. The world was different since his time with the sirens. The sun was brighter, he imagined stars, and the times when night turned to day had become riots of color.

Just as his bleary eyes were focusing on the light growing in the East, one of the creatures came into view. She had auburn hair and black eyes. A patch of downy tan feathers adorned her shoulders like a shawl. In other circumstances, he would have thought she was an angel. He called her Rena. He had watched her and her sisters pull men from the ocean. Some lived for a few days; he knew from their low moans that they shared his fate, injured and slowly succumbing to infection. The rest, the dead ones, the sirens had dismantled with inhuman efficiency and consumed.

Sometimes the beasts brought him food or water. Other times, they took things from him.

Bacchus watched helplessly as Rena leaned over his wound. Her mouth opened wide-too wide-and then she bit down over the knife wound with small, sharp teeth. The pain was immense, almost as much as the first stab. However, he knew that when she finished the oozing pus would be gone, as well as more of his blood.

Sometimes they came to bleed his leg, other times they came to remove different fluids. Neither was enjoyable, no matter how seductive their song. But he couldn't help himself. He was a man, and despite the monstrous details up close, they were still the most beautiful faces he had ever seen. Their beauty and their song ripped at his heart. Their melodies were more alluring than the sounds of the sea. The sirens enticed him despite the pain they brought.

He gritted his teeth but remained silent as Rena sucked his life away.

He loved her, even as she hurt him.

He loved them all; loved them more than he loved his ship. Or himself.

Bacchus squinted into the brightness of the rising sun and wondered if this was an effect from the sirens. Maybe it was fever and madness. Rena finished and licked her scarlet lips, and then he fell asleep.

Dissent

"It's madness," said Rhys, Kurian's only other surviving friend. "The man's dead."

"I would agree with you," Kurian said, "except for the visions."

"This is new for you," Rhys sounded accusing and jabbed a finger at Kurian. "How do you know they're real?"

"I've had the same dreams," added Tobin.

Kurian had brought his closest circle into his childhood home to tell them what he intended to do. Louise Prescott, the spy for the King of the Caves who had been their guide, was skeptical. Her friend Gideon seemed indifferent. Sage Bennet and Ward Finlay, the ancient Capric monks who had risen from their tombs during the battle, were reserved. Rhys was indignant.

"Couldn't this just be guilt?" Louise asked.

"It's as if I'm seeing through his eyes," Kurian answered. Tobin agreed.

"You are certain the man sees the sun in the vision?" asked Sage. "You told us the sky was dark your whole lives." Kurian and Tobin both nodded.

Ward grunted. "Then it's a true vision. There's confirmation within the details, and with Tobin."

"But we've all seen the sun," Rhys said. "His mind is putting it in the dream."

"You're not the King's man yet. You won't fully understand," Ward said with an unusual softness in his tone. "If the King is leading Kurian in this direction, he must go."

"What do we do?" wondered Kurian.

"What is right?" Sage asked in reply.

"Exactly," Rhys said. "You've just routed Evasius, but he's still out there. You can't leave for a month! He'll come right back and kill everyone here."

Ward Finlay, the first protector of the treasure, spoke up. "Normally, I would agree with Rhys. It's poor strategy to abandon your people after a big win, and with the threat of this Evasius still looming over us. But when the King calls, you go. If our enemy lost as much as I believe he did, he won't muster any resistance, nor be a hazard before spring."

"Thank you for your counsel, all of you," Kurian said. He looked at Rhys, standing so tall over the hearth. Rhys kept shaking his head. None of this made sense to him. It broke Kurian's heart, but for the first time in their journey, the three friends couldn't agree on their course. He and Tobin had changed too much after their encounter with the King of the Caves. Rhys had to stay behind.

Kurian looked at Sage for confirmation and felt there was agreement in his gaze. He knew Tobin was on board and that everyone in the room waited for his decision. He cleared his throat. "A small group will go and try against everything we know to save him."

He chose Louise, Sage, and Tobin to go with him to Whalesand, the port town where they had hired Captain Bacchus to take them across Syrene Bay.

Kurian caught Rhys's arm as he stormed out of the door. "This is nothing against you," Kurian whispered. "I'm leaving you to secure Viviford with your heroes, Ward Finlay, and Gideon."

Rhys nodded once and stomped out.

Louise was the first to speak again. "None of you have mentioned the obvious."

"Which is?" Ward asked.

"How are all of *you*," she answered, gesturing at them, "going to rescue a man from an island that devours men?"

Kurian and Tobin looked down, silent.

"Maybe we should call for a few of the women from the King's camp," Louise suggested.

"Not enough women in camp," Gideon said. "Few of them trained. And too long to retrieve them." Everyone saw the condescending look Louise leveled at him.

"He's right," Kurian spoke up. "We need to go with what we have. Time is too short."

"The King knows our need," Sage said. "He sent the visions. He'll provide what help we require. It may well be the women you have in mind, Miss Prescott."

Visitation

The surreal experiences increased by the day, usually with the first light. This morning, the bright light in the east burned through Bacchus' eyelids, waking him again. He shifted his position to sit against a log and squinted into the strange but beautiful dawn. It warmed him slightly in the dewy air. The sirens had made the entire world more glorious as it tried to live up to their beauty.

A silhouette approached in the light, but it wasn't a female form. It wasn't one of his lovers.

Jealousy flared immediately into rage, and Bacchus moved to stand. His left calf felt numb and wouldn't hold him. The pain that shot through his thigh and into his groin crumpled him to the ground.

"No need to stand," said the figure in the light.

When Bacchus looked up, the delirium worsened. The figure itself was the light rising from the east, and the sky—the entire world—dimmed in the light from this shining being.

"They're mine!" Bacchus roared. He grabbed a nearby stick and swung wildly from his stomach.

"I know you're not ready to hear it," said the man made of light, "but help will be here soon."

Bacchus swung again and shouted, "Get out of here!" Then he lost all strength, and his head dropped onto the sand and rocks. He huffed and sand scattered in his breath.

He heard a chirping, but he couldn't tell where it came from. He closed his eyes hard, and when he opened them, he was alone. Only the garish morning light remained. Sharp nails dug into his skin as strong hands grabbed his arm and dragged him back to his spot by the log. The hands dropped him, so his face landed next to a torn open pomegranate and a mealy apple. He rolled and looked up into the golden-brown eyes of a siren. She squawked at him angrily, then returned to the forest. Bacchus waited until his breathing slowed, then flung an arm over his eyes and fell back asleep.

Whalesand

Kurian consulted with his friends during the journey. He still worried that his vision was only wishful thinking. Guilt lingered about the fate of Captain Bacchus. Sage and Tobin reassured him about their mission.

Tobin and Kurian spent much of the trip trying to pry stories from Sage about his life in the misty past of the Kingdom of Fin. They wondered how many of the legends were true. He always delayed their inquiries by saying, "Later, we will have time for tale weaving. First, I need to understand what's happening here and now." When they asked where he had been since his death, he gazed into the distance and smiled. "Later."

Tobin did not hesitate to tell Sage what they knew of the history of their monastic order, the rule of the Evasians, and the darkness that lingered over Pallingham for generations.

"This is true?" Sage asked one evening during sunset, "You had never seen the sun or the stars? The river ceased to flow?" All three of the youths confirmed it.

"Astonishing," Sage said. The next day, he began teaching them how to use the sun and stars to find their direction.

The trip to Whalesand took over two weeks. They arrived in Whalesand just before dark on the sixteenth day, riding up to the Blubber and Bone, the low-arched building said to be framed with whale ribs. When they entered, the innkeeper treated them much as he had the first time, serving oily fish stew and very little information.

However, they immediately recognized Mr. Darling, sitting at the same table the crew of the Osprey had previously occupied. The scene was quiet and subdued, not the continual celebration they had observed under Cpt. Bacchus' leadership.

Kurian approached first, thanking Mr. Darling for his previous service, and telling him how they desired to rescue Cpt. Bacchus.

"He's dead," was all Mr. Darling would say.

Kurian tried to explain why he thought Cpt. Bacchus was alive, and to ask for help. The rhyming duo, Bill and Sam, looked up with hope during Kurian's story. Mr. Darling shook his head and repeated, "He's dead."

"You must help us," Kurian pleaded. When there was no answer, he asked, "How did you resist the sirens so well?"

Mr. darling looked Kurian in the eye for the first time. "I'm mostly deaf, lad. When Dilly got the wax in my ears, I couldn't hear aught." Then he gazed solemnly at Kurian before saying, "Dilly's dead. I won't face those creatures again for him. Not at the risk of my crew and my ship."

"He was your captain," Tobin said.

Mr. Darling's jaw clenched. "He was my partner. The crew fears me; they revered him. They wouldn't follow me into the jaws of that song again." He rose from the table and left through the back hallway before anyone spoke again.

That settled it. Bacchus' crew would not help, despite rhyming complaints from Bill and Sam. Kurian knew no other captain would face the sirens in this place.

Louise was listening from a side table. Her gray-green eyes blazed with disgust. When the conversation ended, she went out the front door.

Siblings

ouise left the Blubber and Bone and walked the short distance to the shoreline. The low sun glared over the horizon, silhouetting the ships docked on the pier a hundred yards down the shore. A bright crescent moon stood above the island across the water. Sounds of distant voices and creaking wood drifted to her on the cold ocean breeze from the pier. She didn't know what the men had experienced as they sailed past the sirens, but she was certain that Mister Darling's excuses were cowardice. She watched him walking toward his ship, the Osprey.

During the trip to Whalesand, she had a growing feeling that Kurian's visions were true, which meant there was a life at stake. She could hardly endure the practical calculations of a man with no heart and no hope for people under his protection.

As she strode the beach praying, she noticed a shape in the water near the island. It looked like a small boat, but it was nearer the island than any of the others would go, impossibly so. Louise watched the boat returning as the sun set and darkness fell. She needed to know who was in that boat.

Stars were dotting the sky, and the moon was the only illumination when she heard the ongoing chatter of a young woman above the methodical splashing and dripping of oars.

"Oy," said the voice as the boat drew close. "Can you help us pull up the beach?"

"Yes," Louise called. She met the prow of a small fishing boat at the edge of the water and pulled with all her strength. The boat lodged in the sand. Two pairs of feet splashed in the lapping tide.

A girl of about fifteen landed on Louise's side with tangled blond hair that reflected the moonlight. Her round eyes teared in the salty breeze, and her small face and narrow jaw made them look big and bright. She wore short-legged pants and a baggy, light-colored tunic that could not have kept out the cold. On the other side, stood a young man. He wore similar clothes, except that his tunic had no sleeves and billowed in the wind. His hair was also tangled, but not as blond, and his face shared the same narrow jaw, tapering to a pointing chin. His arms were gangly but strung with cords of muscle.

"Oh," said the girl, looking up, "a stranger. You don't have to help us."

The young man looked at Louise once, then reached into the boat and dragged out a small net full of large fish.

"It's no problem," Louise said. "Only tell me what to do."

The girl shrugged and pointed. "Lift it and walk it over there." The three of them grabbed the boat by the outside rail and lifted. The boat was as heavy as Louise expected. The wood bit into her hands, but she felt as though the others were doing most of the work without her. They walked the boat up the beach to the other small boats resting in the grass above and rolled it over to drain.

"Thank you," the girl said when they were done.

Louise followed the pair as they each picked up one side of the net of fish. "It's no trouble," Louise said. "What had you out so late after the other boats?"

"Just trying to fill the net," the girl said with a shrug and half smile. "It's the only way we eat."

Louise could see the question made her uncomfortable. She decided to change the subject. "Your brother doesn't say much."

"How did you..." the girl began, then shrugged again. "We do look almost like a mirror." Louise strained to hear her mumbling over the lapping water and their footsteps crunching in the sand.

"I'm Louise."

The girl hesitated, then shifted her grip on the net. "Mercia," she said only glancing toward Louise.

"And your brother?"

She glanced at him before saying, "Ham." Ham continued to gaze forward, ignoring Louise and their conversation.

Louise tried to feign ignorance. "Everyone here says the island is so dangerous, but it looked like you rowed fairly close with no trouble. Are the stories just myths?"

"We're different," Mercia said forcefully. Then she thanked Louise again and quickened her pace. Ham had to catch up with the sudden change. Louise jogged after them.

"Different how?" Mercia ignored her as well as Ham had. Louise followed them almost to the pier before speaking plainly. "I know I'm a stranger, and it's not my right to ask about your life, but my friends and I need help. And if you can get near that island without harm, then you may be the only chance we have."

Mercia tugged on the net and stopped. Ham stopped, looked at her, and held up his free hand in silent question. She held her hand up to him in a "stop" gesture, then looked at Louise.

"We can pay you," Louise added.

"Why on earth would you want to go near that island?"

"To help someone in trouble."

For a moment, there was a look of sympathy in Mercia's face. "If they're on the island, they're dead already."

"We have confidence he's alive," Louise said defensively.

Mercia dropped the net and stepped close to Louise, her gaze suddenly intense. "We go to that island because it's the only place we don't get crowded out by the other boats. It's the only place left where we can make a catch big enough to live on. That secret's been very hard to keep since the sun came out. Going near the island has only made our neighbors hate us more. And every day that we go, I see those creatures on the shore. I hear their squawking that men find so irresistible. Lately, I've heard the piteous moans of their victims. And I've seen what the monsters do to them." Mercia's face was flushed. She took a deep, wavering breath and shook her head. "If you have a friend there, pray he died quickly. There's no hope to survive."

"We have hope." Louise wiped her eyes.

"Then you're fools." Mercia picked up the net again. "We have a catch to sell."

"How does your brother resist their song?"

"Ask him yourself."

Louise looked at him, still staring ahead to the ships at the pier, apparently ignoring the entire conversation. The hand gestures suddenly made sense. "He's deaf."

Mercia feigned applause.

"Would you at least hear us out?" Louise asked. "We'll pay for the fish."

Mercia tugged the net again. When Ham looked, she made several signals, including pointing to Louise, the island, and the fish. Ham's gaze rested on Louise for only the second time. After studying her face for a moment, he held out an open hand, then touched two fingers under his eyes. Louise thought she understood: he wanted to see the money.

Help

Louise strode back toward the Blubber and Bone with Mercia and Ham when someone called her name. She turned to see a boy running to her from the road.

"Crispin?" she shouted.

"Another stranger," Mercia whispered behind her.

"Just a boy," Louise whispered.

A smile spread across Crispin's whole face as he neared. His long brown curls bounced with each step. He finished with a leap, landing inches from Louise.

"What are you doing here?" Louise asked.

"Xander sent me," he beamed. "He told me to find our people."

"Alone?"

"I'm almost eleven," he said, standing tall. "You traveled alone when you were my age. Xander told me."

It was true, but it seemed different to her seeing a child going on a mission after she had years of service to the King. She couldn't argue, so she shrugged her shoulders. "I suppose you're right on time, then."

Crispin's smile rolled out like a scroll. Then he wrinkled his nose. "What's that smell?"

"That is the sweet scent of the ocean," Mercia said, smiling. But her tone was full of sarcasm.

"Or it's the stew from the inn," Louise said under her breath as she opened the door.

Negotiations

Kurian looked up when the door opened and was surprised to see Louise with three others. He recognized the boy walking closely by her side from the King's camp, but the other two were from Whalesand. He noticed other patrons giving them suspicious glances.

Louise introduced everyone, then insisted they pay for the net of fish that Mercia and Ham carried.

"Why do we need fish?" Kurian asked.

"Because I offered to buy them in exchange for listening to us," Louise said. "I believe they can help."

Sage said, "Didn't I tell you the King would send what help we require?"

"We'll see," Kurian said. Turning to Ham, he asked, "How much for the fish?"

Mercia gave him a price, and Kurian handed it over. Then he called the owner to the table and haggled with him over using the fish as payment for their stay. Finally, he turned back to the siblings. "How can you help us?"

"We haven't agreed to," Mercia replied. Kurian hadn't expected her to answer again, while Ham only glanced from face to face, not seeming to follow who was talking.

Louise leaned in and spoke into his ear. "They fish at the island." Kurian stared at her, waiting, knowing she had waited until her preferred moment to give him all the information. "Ham can't hear," she added.

"So, like Mister Darling, the sirens don't affect him," Kurian said in a low voice.

Mercia nodded. "They're terrible enough for me, though. Thank you for asking."

"Did Louise tell you why we're here?"

She nodded again.

"Are you willing to help?" Tobin asked, hopeful.

Mercia shook her head, aghast. "Why should we? I told her your friend is dead."

"We have good reason to believe he lives," Sage said, leaning forward.

The fire crackled loudly beside their table while they waited for Mercia to answer. Conversations from other tables seemed to hush in the pause. Crispin's gaze leapt from face to face, much like Ham's. Kurian thought he could read the questions in the boy's eager expression. Mercia made a few gestures back and forth with her brother, then swept her tangled hair over her shoulder, and played with the ends.

"I don't know how we could help," she said. "We've been near the island, not on it. I'm sure those beasts would tear you apart for landing there."

"You said you've heard men there," Louise whispered. "How long ago?"

Mercia closed her eyes tightly for a moment. "Maybe two days."

"It could be him," Kurian said.

"It could be your friend," she said grimly, "as they eat him."

"What would it take for you to help us?" Tobin asked softly.

"I wish that I could help the men who I've heard." Mercia's voice wavered, and tears began to fall. She moved her hands as she spoke through this part, and her brother watched. "Even if it were to ease their deaths. But I won't risk my brother to those monsters." Nobody answered.

"And how do you expect to get within a half mile of the island yourselves?" she asked. "You're men, and you can hear."

"Not me," Crispin chirped. He blushed when everyone looked at him. "Well, I'm not a man."

Kurian felt his stomach turn as he remembered the siren song. But something deep within urged him to answer boldly. He struggled to find words that could express why they hoped to rescue Bacchus. He didn't think she could understand what the river waters had done to them, or what the King's voice was like inside his spirit. He settled for what sounded to him like brash overconfidence.

"We're different," he said with a level gaze at Mercia. Her inhospitable shell cracked. A log crumbled in the fireplace and she flinched.

Louise smiled. "Have you heard about the river yet, and Evasius' defeat?" she whispered.

"Tales," Mercia balked and moved her hands for Ham.

"No," Tobin said. "We were there. We defeated Evasius."

Mercia laughed. "All five of you?"

"We had a lot of help," Kurian said.

"What do you know of the old stories of Fin and King Frederick?" Sage asked, stroking his chin.

Afloat

They had stayed up late into the night discussing what Mercia and Ham knew about the sirens and the island, then planned their approach. They slept most of the day, then late in the afternoon, after Mr. Darling extorted half their coin for a second small boat, they pushed off from shore. Sage and Tobin rode with Ham and Mercia while Kurian and Crispin rowed alongside with Louise. A trio of ships stood silhouetted outside the mouth of the bay. The air was calm, making the moment seem frozen. Only the gulls and the rhythmic dipping of the oars in the water gave a sense of time.

"Last chance to back out," Louise said quietly to Kurian. "You think you can withstand them?"

"Having you with me worked best last time," Kurian said.

"Only because we tackled you."

He blushed. "Crispin's still too young for the worst effects, I expect. I only hope the creatures aren't strong."

"Let me know if you need help," Louise said to Crispin. He nodded and turned toward the prow. His eyes scanned the island.

"You're certain they're less active before sunset, Mercia?" Kurian asked.

"They seem to have been with us," she called from the other boat. "But they might've grown accustomed to us coming every day."

"So, you think they might not notice our arrival?" Tobin asked.

"They can't miss us if you don't cover up," she teased. Tobin pulled the collar of his cloak together as if she had discovered him shirtless. Kurian did the same. With each stroke at the oars, he saw the glare beneath his collar. They both wore the armor they had received from the King, and it gleamed in the sunlight like a torch at night. Sage wore his dull, ancient mail, and Louise had donned a thick, leather tunic.

"And you've only seen a dozen on the beach?" Kurian asked.

"Yes," Mercia answered with some aggravation, "but they may not have been the same ones."

"If you're scared, we can turn back," she added, with hand gestures. Ham shook his head sternly. "I'd go back, but my brother can't refuse your price."

"Thank you again for helping us," said Kurian.

Mercia pointed toward the island. "You can see the cove better now. It's deep enough to anchor out of the tide, but close enough to swim back if the sirens kill most of you."

They were nearly halfway between shores. After discussing the details of the cove for a moment, Kurian, Sage, and Tobin plugged their ears with wax, as Captain Bacchus' crew had done. To improve the protection from the Song, they placed thick wool pads over their ears and wrapped bandages around their heads to secure them. As Crispin wrapped the gauze under Kurian's chin, and over his head, the sounds of the oars and the water lapping against the boats faded beneath the sound of his breathing. When Crispin asked how it was working, it sounded as if he were speaking through a pillow. It was no louder than a whisper.

The silence left Kurian primarily with his thoughts, and memories of the sirens tried to flood his mind. He focused as intensely as he could on the vision, remembering the pain and confusion, the terror of the sirens themselves. They were here to save Captain Bacchus. Kurian hoped it would be enough purpose to help him fight back against the Song.

He tried to anchor his mind on what he had told Mercia: they were different. The King and the water of the river had made them something other than ordinary men. He knew it was true, even though he did not fully understand what it all meant, or how it all worked. Sage had pulled him aside with Tobin before they boarded the boats and encouraged them in that. "You were right to say you are different," he said, barely audible over the rolling tide. "The King has called you. And changed you. These beasts we go to are not simply wild; they are creatures of darkness, and darkness does not live in you anymore. They will try to attack your heart and your mind, the weakness that may yet remain. But you are new, and those weaknesses have been conquered by a power that their evil does not understand. You can resist and fight back. Stand firm in the name of the King."

That memory settled Kurian's mind most of all. He craned his neck to see Sage in the other boat, deep in prayer. Just over Sage's shoulder, Kurian saw the island looming near, and he noticed the Song, hovering at the edge of hearing.

Landing

"What's that horrible sound?" Crispin asked, the words muffled and hard to hear. Kurian found the disgust in his face amusing.

"That is the siren song," Louise answered.

"It sounds like a cat fight on top of a grinding stone." Crispin cringed. Mercia and Louise agreed.

"That's not what we hear," Tobin said distantly.

Crispin studied Tobin's face. "It's horrible," he said, "but I can see how you think it's interesting. Like picking at a scab."

"Enough talk," Sage said, and everyone fell silent.

With each pull of the oars, the shore crept closer, and the Song grew louder. Rowing distracted Kurian. Having Louise in the boat helped, too. But there was also a deep resolve to resist inside him as Sage had told him. However, Kurian wavered between looking and not looking. His imagination of what was happening on the island behind him ran wild as he remembered the distant forms on the beach from their previous close encounter with the sirens. But the physical work at the oars gave him enough focus to keep his head. Still, every few strokes, he glanced over his shoulder. Each time, the trees were larger, and the cove nearer. At first, he saw a few sirens come out on the sand, dancing and calling, but as they continued their approach without the wild abandon the creatures were used to, they retreated and hid. Nobody spoke as they came within a quarter mile of the island, or Kurian could not hear any words. The siren song was still a whisper compared to their time on the Osprey. When they were one hundred yards from the shore, there was only light movement at the tree line beyond the beach. Then, all the clues of the siren's presence vanished.

The sun had dipped low, touching the horizon. It would set in moments. The southern point of the cove covered it before it sank into the sea. The heavy timber on the west side of the island plunged them into shadow as the first boat skidded against the sand. Louise and Crispin stepped out and splashed in the water. Kurian stowed the oars and joined them on the beach. They threw a line to Mercia, who tied their boat to the stern of her own.

Before they knew how the sirens would react, Ham landed the second boat to their right. Sage jumped out first, overstepping the water somehow, and not making a sound. He grabbed the prow of the boat and kneeled low. Tobin stepped out beside him and scanned the trees, ready to draw his sword. Mercia also exited the boat. As one of the few who could swim, Ham waited until Sage pushed him back into the tide, so he could pull away from the shore and anchor the boats out of reach.

They clustered close together, watching the tree line, and waiting for Ham to return.

"I thought you were waiting in the boats," Kurian said to Mercia.

She gave him a fierce look and said, "My brother wants a crack at one of those things."

Louise touched her shoulder. "They're dangerous. You mustn't risk your lives for our mission. You don't have to do this!"

"Yes, we do," Mercia said after glancing back toward her brother.

The moon was rising above one hill like a dimly glowing horn. In the silence, everything in Kurian's ears was the Song. It tickled his ears, and the longer he listened, the more pleasant it seemed to become.

There was a warmth in his heart. He felt light, almost giddy. He suddenly recognized how intense his affection was for everyone there on the beach with him. He wanted to hug Tobin, to sit at Sage's feet and listen for hours. Even Mercia was a fine young woman he could appreciate. But Louise...

When he gazed on Louise, he felt stupid for not pursuing such a beautiful woman. As he studied her dark hair and stormy gray-green eyes, a thought occurred to him: *I'm a king now. She would make a wonderful queen.* He leaned in closer, intending to ask her opinion about his brilliant idea, but before he could ask, he found that his lips were already mashed tightly against hers. He was kissing her, and it was delicious until she sputtered and pushed him away. The sting of her slap brought their purpose back into focus. He heard a laugh from Mercia and then splashing behind him as Ham made it ashore.

Sage held up a hand, signaling them to wait. After what felt like several long minutes, a single form stepped out onto the beach some distance to the right. They all stared without a word. In the dimness, Kurian could only distinguish the tall, slender shape of a woman. The dark hid many of the details, but the soft curves of breast and hips triggered an immediate reaction within him. Louise was nothing now. His body ached to be close to the vision in the twilight. He desired to touch the skin that seemed to have its own radiance, like the moon. The Song intensified, bypassing his ears and going straight to his head, and into his heart. Breathing became difficult. Then the images began, like last time. Memories first, then promises of what that body could do. Once again, he felt the secret thrill and shame of each new idea.

Tobin let out a small whine. Then a giggle.

In Kurian's peripheral vision, Sage drew his sword. "Resist," he said firmly.

It was enough to give Kurian's resolve a foothold. He threw off his cloak, revealing his armor. It seemed to draw the last remaining light to itself, a glimmering beacon in the fading dusk. From his back, he pulled his shield with the King's symbol. The figure by the forest startled and stepped back. Finally, he drew his sword from its scabbard, its deadly edge hissing in the quiet. The siren ran into the darkness.

With the siren gone, Tobin turned his head to Mercia, then blushed. He looked like a drunk who had lost control of his face. In jerking motions, he lifted his eyes like a scared puppy and threw Mercia a pleading, twitching smile. Ham eyed Tobin suspiciously.

"No," Mercia said, shaking her head and pointing a finger. Tobin drew his head down between his shoulders. "You're not turning that lust toward me just because the screaming bird-woman ran off into the woods."

"Bird-woman?" Tobin laughed.

"Yeah," said Mercia, her eyes opening wide. "You'll see when we get closer."

"We know," Kurian growled.

Tobin looked where the siren had stood and smiled again. He sighed, "Closer," and took off at a full sprint in the direction she had gone.

Ambush

Kurian charged after Tobin. He heard Louise and Sage behind him, both shouting, "Stop!"

He assumed they thought he was under the sirens' spell like Tobin. Behind him, Louise shouted again, "Tobin, Kurian, stop. It's an ambush!"

Tobin didn't stop, so Kurian continued. The ambush was obvious, but he had to reach Tobin before he reached the trees.

The sand pulled at his feet, sapping his speed and balance. Meanwhile, the Song strengthened with every step.

They were ten yards from the timberline, and the noise sounded almost like a frenzy, but Kurian ignored it for the sake of his best friend. He knew the creatures were waiting just inside the shadow of the forest.

He finally overcame Tobin a few steps into the shadows and pushed him to the ground. Something leapt at him from the right. There was a momentary glimpse of large, leathery feet with sharp claws, but he was already swinging his sword. It connected, and he skidded to a stop. Kurian heard a heavy thud behind him and then horrible squeals, like those from an injured animal. A step behind him was a large bird foot, severed above the spur.

Between him and Tobin lay a nude woman grabbing her leg, cut off mid-calf. The other leg lay at an odd angle, as if the knee were backward. It had a taloned foot. Her face clenched in pain for a moment, and then she opened her mouth unnaturally wide and let out a deafening, inhuman wail of agony and rage. Kurian's revulsion was immediate. The song's spell broke. He saw the disgust on Tobin's face for an instant before another siren crashed through the trees.

She lunged at Kurian and swiped with one of her taloned feet. He dodged and parried a second attack. A hand darted out, and the smaller talons scraped across his breastplate. Kurian waited for the next leap and aimed his sword for her heart.

The creature shrieked and scratched at him a moment, then faded. Before he could clear her off the blade, another was on him. Their radiant skin stood out enough in the dark to allow him a chance at defending himself. A fourth attacked Tobin, and Kurian realized the bird-women surrounded him. Their friends caught up; Sage dispatched the siren leaping for Tobin. Louise and Crispin both held small swords. Ham wielded his long knife for cleaning fish, while his sister had a net and a large fish bat.

Suddenly, the forest came alive with movement. Bushes shook, and sirens appeared out from every direction. Kurian heard Sage shouting orders, but he couldn't make out what was said. Two or three horrors swarmed him at once. He saw that they were pushing to isolate him. He fought hard to get closer, but more of the beasts jumped between him and his friends. They swiped and slashed with animal ferocity. He would have rather battled a pack of wolves.

Three sirens stood directly in front of Kurian, ready to pounce, while two more flanked him on either side. The notion came to him to pray like Sage had when they fought Lord Evasius, but another part of him thought, *what's the point? You're about to die.*

Help would be nice, he thought to the voice that had been so present in their last battle. A siren lurched forward on his left. He blocked with his shield, then swung at the attack from the right.

A light grew behind the sirens before him. He was about to thank the King for a new miracle when a flaming fishing net dropped onto his foes.

They shrieked and writhed in panic. Each tried to flee but fell in the binding. The foes at his flank stopped, then retreated into the darkness. Kurian quickly killed two in the net, and Ham took out the third. He spat on them, then stomped back to Mercia with a look of pride.

The others all stood in a loose oval, facing outward, ready to fight. Eighteen sirens lay dead or dying on the ground. The wounded clawed and bit weakly at their enemies, ignoring their wounds. Sage methodically ended their agony.

"Everyone still here?" Louise called.

"Yes," Kurian answered. He rejoined the circle. Crispin and Mercia were already making torches. Reaching out, Kurian touched Ham's shoulder and said, "Thank you." Ham nodded.

"You owe us a net," Mercia said, holding out a torch to light.

Regroup

When everyone had a torch, they turned northeast and walked deeper into the forest. "Why are we going this way?" Crispin asked.

Louise said, "Because the sirens went through the trees the other way."

"How do you know that?" asked Tobin.

Mercia glared at him. "We still have our ears, heartbreaker."

"It's also the direction of the beach that Bacchus probably made it to, Crispin," said Kurian over his shoulder. He held his sword in one hand and the torch in the other as he led them through the wood. A network of trails crossed their path frequently, but Kurian kept on the same course.

Crispin rubbed his temples and asked, "Do we have any more of those ear stoppers? Their noise is giving me a headache."

The song continued throughout their trek, but it had changed, taken on a new tone. It became more torture than allure. Where it had once crept into Kurian's mind with promises and dreams of illicit pleasure, now it attacked his senses with pain.

Louise reached into a satchel slung over her shoulder and handed Crispin some wax. She took some for herself and offered it to Mercia. Mercia shook her head.

"Crispin's right," said Kurian. "It's not lust and desire anymore, but pain. It doesn't draw me to find the source. Instead, it feels like I'm hurt and sick, body and soul."

"The song is drastically different," Tobin said. "It feels like the discomfort after overindulging in a meal."

Kurian stopped for a moment in a large intersection. When they had bunched together, Sage patted Tobin on the back. "That's much worse than overeating, Tobin. That pain is their loss and grief. We killed many of them. It reminds me of men I knew, soldiers mostly, men who tried to live the type of life the sirens sang to us at first. It's a grief I wished I might never have to see again."

"How do we find your friend so we can get off this island?" Mercia asked, irritated.

"It isn't that big," Kurian said before continuing on their path. "First, we check the beach we saw from his ship."

Mercia pushed a branch out of her way. "But they could hide him anywhere in this."

"You're assuming they think as we do," Tobin said from behind. Kurian knew the tone. Mercia was about to get a lecture. "As far as we can tell, they're more animal than human. Nobody who has ever come here resisted them. Imagine if a fly suddenly landed in a spider's web and fought back with something as strange to the spider as fire is to the sirens. The spider would most likely run in fear, but then look for new ways to catch its prey."

"How's that help us find him?" Crispin asked.

"Wonderful! More reason to be afraid," Mercia said with fake enthusiasm.

Tobin cleared his throat. "They've likely never had to worry about hiding anything, except maybe from each other. But since they appear to work together, they most likely don't."

Kurian stopped. Judging distances in the thick timber was hard. He felt like they had only walked a half-mile, but it could be as little as a few hundred yards. Ahead of him, a rock face about nine feet tall ended their current path. From the water, it had looked like a low, gradual hill, but the trees concealed the wall near the base. The path was clear along the rock face going east. To his left, it jogged around a corner and turned up the hill on a more reasonable slope. The paths made sense the way rabbit and mouse trails did in the grass on the plains. They used the shortest, easiest route to what they wanted.

He turned to Sage and said, "At least we won't have to worry about danger from all directions for a bit."

Sage walked to the front. He glanced back at Kurian and shook his head, then took the lead, alert.

They walked silently and slowly along the trail for another twenty yards. Kurian was certain the sirens knew where they were, no matter how carefully they moved. He kept his back close to the wall so he could see threats coming from the forest. In the light of Sage's torch, he saw where the stone drew away from them, bending north. The turn was sharper than he thought, essentially a corner. Sage sped up as he rounded it. Kurian hurried to keep up. He passed a deep cleft in the rock when he heard the snap of a breaking branch. They stopped and peered into the tree line.

Strong claws yanked Kurian into the heavy shadows behind him. He dropped the torch. The siren whirled him around, and he fell face first to the dirt.

He pushed up, but the creature landed on him. It shrieked, scratching at the shield on his back.

Getting his arms under him to push again, he saw two more sirens drop from above. One of them tried to stomp on his torch and fell back screaming. The other crouched to pounce on him, but Sage cut it down.

Kurian heaved upward, knocking the siren against the roof. From his knees, he swung the sword blindly. Only the dull sound of it hitting flesh and the muffled scream told him he connected.

His friends were still fighting when he raced out of the cave. Sirens leapt from the trees and from the cliff above. In their fury, they no longer looked like nude women, but demons ready to devour their prey. Only the torches tempered their ferocity. They recoiled from the flames as more flocked around his friends. Soon there would be too many.

"In here!" he shouted above the chaos. Then he knocked down an enemy advancing on Mercia and pushed the girl toward the hole in the rocks. Sage defended the entrance. One by one, Kurian helped them break off their fights, or kill their adversaries, and they retreated into the dark behind Sage. As he backed toward Sage's side, he picked up his own torch. The creatures gathered in a loose arc just out of reach. Sage and Kurian advanced, swinging torch and sword, pushing them back. Then they returned to the entrance while the sirens hovered outside the circle of light. Their horrible Song was deafening, despite the wax and bandages over Kurian's ears.

Louise brought forward an armful of branches and twigs and dropped them at the cave's mouth. She spent a few moments arranging the kindling, and then Tobin held two torches against the pile until they caught. The sirens retreated further. Ham and Mercia piled on more wood until there was a bright fire.

"Sage," Kurian said. "Thank you for taking point at the wall. I didn't see the danger."

Sage bowed his head, still breathing heavily. "We were no longer exposed on every flank. But threats from the left became threats from above." Kurian nodded. Sage smiled gently. "King Frederick received council humbly. It's a good sign that you can, too."

"Council inside, gentlemen," Louise said. "I'll take guard duty. You find us a way out of here." When Sage and Kurian stepped into the cave, the sirens screeched even louder but kept to the border between light and shadow.

Respite

The torchlight revealed a small cave. The rear wall held a tangle of branches and leaves that reminded Kurian of a nest. Tobin pulled more kindling from it and dropped it near the fire. Ham and Mercia sat against the wall on the right. Both had looks of anger and horror. Ham gawked at the corpse that Kurian had killed in the dark. Mercia stared at Kurian. Sage quickly picked up the body to carry it out. He tossed it over the fire, and when it landed at the feet of its kin, they shrieked again and skittered toward the forest. Between Louise, the fire, and their dead sister, the sirens did not seem eager to attack again. However, the song continued with the mournful pain that had been going on since their first skirmish.

"That tidies the place a little," Sage said after returning. Tobin pulled sticks from the nest, studying it the whole time, while Crispin climbed in and sat cross-legged.

Mercia waved her hands in intricate patterns to her brother. He made significantly fewer gestures in return. Mostly, he shook his head. After a moment, Mercia pounded her fists on her knees and yelled in frustration. "Why are we here, Kurian? This is what I was afraid of: that we'd be overrun and die here."

He didn't know how to answer. Things looked bleak. They had not found Bacchus yet. The sirens were smart hunters and had them trapped. However, they had successfully repelled the creatures' attacks. Quickly, he prayed for guidance but heard nothing over the constant noise of the song. It slowed every thought and battered his senses like waves on a rock. He had only his intuition to confront Mercia's exaggeration head on.

"But we haven't been overrun," he said, "and we're not dead."

Mercia stood and pointed her finger in his face. "We're stuck in a cave!" She screamed. "Dozens of those monsters are waiting to slaughter us. We don't have food. Our water might last a day. The only thing we have is a tiny fire. How long can we hold out?"

"With the size of that nest, we can keep a strong fire well into morning," Tobin offered.

"And then what?" Mercia glared at him.

Kurian stared into her eyes, seeing only fear. She looked like a scared child who had woken to terrors in her bedroom. He had seen the same in novitiates at the monastery, even Tobin on his first night. Beyond the horror of monsters, it was the dread that she would never go home.

"Mercia," he said, softening, "Remember when I told you we were different?"

She stood, huffing out breath after breath of panic.

"How many men have you seen approach this island, let alone stand on it? How many, besides your brother, have resisted the song? Have any men sailed close enough to fire an arrow at the shore, let alone kill a siren?"

"No," she grunted. He could tell she wasn't ready to give up her anger. Her face in the firelight churned with emotion like the sea in a storm.

"We weren't alone in facing Evasius," Kurian told her. "Help arrived precisely when we needed it. That's all I expect you could understand right now. Just know that the one we serve helped us defeat Evasius' army. He made the river flow again. Crispin has seen him overpower a group of soldiers without injuries. Sage...he...well, I don't think you'd believe me if I told you."

"What are you telling me?" Mercia's face was still fearful, but also frustrated.

"If you know the old stories, it should be obvious," Tobin said. "The Apos flows, the gloom has gone, and there's a king in Pallingham again."

"How does that help us now?" Mercia screamed again.

"Help will come!" Kurian shouted, but not in anger. Then he lowered his voice and said, "Please give us some time. A way out will become clear."

Mercia shook her head and sat down next to her brother. "You're all insane!"

Watch

Louise watched the forest from beside the fire, angling her body against the rock so she could hear the conversation behind her. She felt a pang of sympathy for Mercia. She remembered feeling alone and afraid before the King found her. Even now she was scared watching the sirens move in to test the light and her defenses. The only difference was she no longer felt alone or lost like she did when she was a girl. She had years of experience serving the King. None of her missions had been so dangerous before Kurian entered the scene, but even that was something the King had prepared her for ahead of time. In the weeks she had known Kurian she often thought about what the King had shown her, and it gave her confidence that they would make it through this ordeal. Still, she wasn't sure she wanted the vision to be her life yet. She felt it coming, but knew it wasn't imminent, and being able to imagine a future gave her time to warm up to it. It also made her feel secure in the danger. There was more after this.

The Song surrounded her like water, bathing her mind in discomfort and pain. The wax only muffled it. However, because it was constant, she found she could ignore it and push it aside. The headache developing from the intense concentration might shorten her ability to function, but she would continue, on alert as long as she could. As the rush from the fight faded, the sword weighed heavy in her hand. She cradled the blade in her other arm to help. Tobin, Kurian, and Sage talked low enough that she couldn't hear them. When she risked a glance back, they were all sitting. Crispin had dozed off.

After a half-hour, Kurian offered to stand guard for her. As soon as he stepped up, the sirens were louder, and they crowded closer to the firelight. Louise took a step forward, and they backed off. She told Kurian she would stay on watch if they supplied food for the flames.

Over an hour later, Louise still stood guard, shifting her weight frequently, and sometimes leaning against the entrance of the cave. Mercia stood up and came near to the fire. The sirens were more subdued faced with only two women.

"How are you holding up?" Louise asked.

"I feel like I'll lose my mind any minute. But I'm more worried about Ham."

Louise saw trails running down the dirt on Mercia's cheeks. She understood. She'd been on the verge of tears multiple times since they stopped moving. There would be many more when she was safe and alone.

Mercia pinched her nose and sniffled. "The Song is so sad, and it hurts. And Ham says he can feel it, despite not hearing it."

"Will he be all right?"

"I hope so," said Mercia, looking over her shoulder. "This whole night was a mistake. He's very tender. It's why he rarely looks at anybody besides me. I'm afraid what this will do to him. If we even make it home." She paused for a moment and looked intently at Louise. "Can we get home? Do you believe Kurian?"

Louise almost laughed, allowing a smile to cross her face. "I've not known him long, but he is tenacious in finding his way through danger. I would say he's protected, and so are those who travel with him. More importantly, I trust the man he's following. Yes, I believe help will come."

Mercia looked more conflicted than relieved. She shivered once in the cold and knelt closer to the fire. When she rose, Louise said, "I'm sorry that we put you in danger."

"I'll accept your apology if we live," Mercia said, then returned to sit beside her brother.

Revelation

Another hour passed. Louise remained on watch. The song never ceased, one moment high, like a mother keening for a dead child, the next low with rage, like a woman discovering an unfaithful lover. The men had rested their weapons on the wall and discussed plans, arguing about how to escape. Their voices sounded more strained with each new idea. Kurian and Tobin asked Sage why he couldn't summon lightning like he had in the battle at Aposford. Sage told them it didn't work like magic; it wasn't him doing *thaumaturgy*. He merely heard what God wanted to do and complied. The Song was getting to him, too, he mentioned, making it hard to hear when he prayed, unlike the familiar sounds of battle.

Louise often felt like that when things were chaotic—as if she were talking to herself instead of praying. Right now, she relied on an undercurrent of peace helping her get through this mess. It was enough to hold her together, but not enough to show her a way out. Worse than the Song itself was that it planted doubt in her mind. She struggled to remember or understand why Kurian wanted to save Cpt. Bacchus. The man was a rogue, arrogant and reckless. She understood Kurian feeling responsible for him being on the island, but she failed to see the purpose in his rescue, except perhaps to ease the guilt. The mission felt too risky for such a selfish reason. *Stop!* She thought. *Fretting about it won't help us escape.*

She shook her head to clear it, and muttered to herself, "You're protecting these people. Focus on your job." She pushed herself off the wall and paced behind the fire, looking for weak points in the sirens' position. They seemed to mill about aimlessly in the dark of the trees. Some squatted, some tittered together like birds. Others preened as they glared into the cave. They all avoided the area around the corpse. Then Mercia began singing. Louise looked over to see Ham resting his head on Mercia's chest.

Her song was quiet and soft. Ham prodded her and she sang louder, but Louise could barely catch the words. It was an unfamiliar lullaby, but even sung quietly, it brought comfort. Louise stopped pacing and kept her ear cocked to listen while she scanned the trees. The men quieted their argument. With her eyes closed, Mercia didn't notice everyone was listening.

Her voice was clear and bright as she carried the simple melody—still a young girl's voice. The lilt in her speech added charm and grace to the song. Ham let out a sigh and visibly re-laxed.

It made Louise realize how tense she had been. She rolled her shoulders, stretched her neck, and took a slow breath.

When she turned back, she couldn't see any sirens. After a moment of searching, she finally saw faint movements deep in the shadows, the reflection of firelight on pale skin. Their song seemed quieter, less enveloping. There were more individual shrieks and titters, instead of the continuous wail it had been.

Louise stared in wonder, then turned and called, "Could you sing louder Mercia?"

Mercia startled and opened her eyes but stopped singing. A deep blush rushed over her freckled cheeks. In her silence, the Song returned with full force.

"Please," Louise said. "It's soothing."

Mercia sang quietly again.

"Louder, please." Louise observed the sirens as Mercia's voice carried. The creatures who had ventured back into the light re-treated again, teeth bared in horrific snarls. Their chorus diminished again. She heard an outbreak of individual noises instead.

"Yes!" Louise shouted and laughed. Her outburst made the men jump. Crispin jerked awake, instantly on his feet. They all looked at her with expectation.

"I think we have a way to fight back!" she said fiercely.

Louise didn't wait for a response, but stepped in front of the fire and sang out:

The night is nearly over; the day is almost here.
Let us lay aside the deeds of darkness, cast away all fear.

Our joy comes with the morning, our waking hour is nigh,
May we bind our hearts with righteousness and lift our eyes on
high."

Reprieve

Kurian stared, shocked at what he saw. Louise sang loudly. She advanced toward the trees, walking with grace and purpose as her voice rang out. The siren song faded. The weight of the horrible noise on his mind lifted, and with it, his whole body felt lighter. He rose to his feet from his knees, wishing he could join in, but he didn't know the lyrics. Crispin had startled awake, and ran forward, joining Louise with enthusiasm. His young voice carried farther and higher than hers. Kurian heard breaking branches as the sirens retreated through the forest. Their song failed altogether, descending to individual cackles and screams before going quiet.

The pair of singers strode back toward the fire as they finished. They shared smiles of relief.

Tobin reached over and pushed Kurian's mouth shut.

"Now we know their weakness," Louise said with a radiant smile. She looked refreshed and alert, even after keeping watch for so long.

Before anyone else spoke, they heard a sound from outside the cave. A cry in the dark silence. It sounded distant, but it was a man's voice in agony, a call for help.

Immediately, the sirens sang out again, covering the voice. This time, they combined their original song of seduction with the painful melancholy of their mourning and rage. It echoed in the cave with fresh vigor, a tumult of noise like two choirs battling in discordant melodies.

"That might have been Bacchus," Kurian shouted.

"It could also be a trap," yelled Tobin.

Mercia stood up and swore. "Did you say Bacchus?"

"Yes."

She stepped so close to Kurian that he backed up. "Captain Bacchus?"

Kurian nodded. She signed something to Ham, then spat on the ground. He rose to his feet, looking angry. She glared at Kurian with eyes so bloodshot they looked infected. They burned with rage. "We're out here risking our lives for that, that lech? Do you know how many girls he's ruined in town? How many people he's cheated for a few coins?"

"He was the only one who helped us in Whalesand," Kurian said.

Mercia sneered. "How much did his *help* cost?"

"That doesn't matter. He's here because of us, and we can only make it right by saving him," Kurian shouted more loudly than before.

"Then we're risking our lives for your guilt." Mercia spat again. "If my brother..."

She stopped when Louise gently touched her shoulder. "I'm sorry this wasn't clear before," Louise said, "but right now, our only hope of getting off this island is staying together. Whatever past you have with Bacchus, save the anger until we're all safe."

"You people are maddening!" Mercia roared, then she stormed to the fire and kicked the sticks toward the trees. A shower of firebrands and sparks scattered the sirens closing in again, and Mercia screamed into the darkness until her breath failed. The sirens screamed back. Ham rushed to her side and pulled her back into the cave. She collapsed into his arms, sobbing.

"We'll get you home safe," Tobin said. "I promise."

Mercia swore at him through her brother's shirt and wept.

Counter-Attack

They spent over an hour trying out different songs and making extra torches to search for the man they had heard. Each new song had an effect, mostly to lighten their spirits. They sampled lullabies and ballads, Mercia tried shanties she heard the sailors singing from their boats, but the sirens only fell silent during the songs that Louise and Crispin knew from the King's camp. Even the hymns that Tobin and Kurian learned at the monastery were less effective.

Kurian noticed Sage's silence and asked, "Don't you have any old songs to sing?"

"You know how ancient they are," Sage smiled. "I think they would sound too strange. Better I learn your new strains." When Kurian asked Louise and Crispin to teach them two of their songs, Sage's voice was strong, but he carried notes longer than the others, and it rolled out with extended vibrato.

The sirens fled again and fell silent immediately when they all sang together, and their melody echoed out from the cave as from an amphitheater. In the quiet moments after, Sage led them in prayer.

"Does everyone have the tunes by heart?" Kurian asked when Sage finished. They all confirmed they did, except Ham.

"If the song works as well out there as from in here, we will spread out and search," Kurian reviewed their final plans. "If you forget the words, hum along until you catch them again. We'll search shoulder to shoulder, Sage on one end, then alternating the stronger fighters—Louise, Tobin, Mercia, Ham, Crispin, then me." Mercia signed to Ham, pointing to each person in turn as Kurian spoke. "Keep your torches high and don't lose sight of each other. If they attack heavily, we move two by two, instead of in line." When their singing stopped, the sirens began their Song again, slowly harmonizing until it saturated the air. Kurian had to shout again to finish. "Mercia, I'd like you and Ham to put the remains of that nest on the fire so we have a landmark in case we must retreat. The rest of us will test the tree line and see if we meet any resistance. Is all of that clear?"

Everyone nodded. "If we find him," Kurian continued, "he's probably injured or weak. How do we get him back to the beach?"

"We could lash branches together and make a sledge like we did when you got stung at Hasslemere," Tobin said.

"Do we have any rope?" Kurian asked.

Louise tapped her shoulder. "I have cordage in my satchel."

"Good," Kurian said. "Can you handle the construction when we find him?"

Louise nodded.

"Are we ready?" Kurian asked.

He looked at their faces. Louise, Sage, and Crispin watched him confidently. Tobin flashed his nervous smile. Mercia looked away when he met her gaze. She shook her head and huffed, "I can't believe I'm doing this." When she saw him still watching her, she relented. "As ready as I can be," she said, shrugging.

"God be with us," Kurian said, then he picked up his sword from against the wall and lit a new torch in the fire. His friends did the same and fanned out between the flames and the forest. Mercia and Ham pushed the nest against the small fire, and it quickly turned into a blaze. Kurian felt the heat rising behind him as the light spread further ahead. What he thought were shadows in the trees were figures that shrank back when illuminated.

He breathed deeply, trying to steady himself for the struggle to come, then he took a final step, right up to the trees and sang out as loudly as he could.

"Call on the Rock, our Fortress, our Shield..."

The others joined in, and their chorus pushed back against the siren's noise.

"The One who gives victory, strength not to yield."

Now he saw a few angry faces from the timbers, but the sirens only screeched and screamed. Their seductive and murderous song failed immediately, and they fled into the darkness. Kurian continued. His own voice filled his head, blocking out all other sounds with his ears plugged.

"Sing to our God, play songs on your lyre,

To Him who will rescue us from death and fire."

A smile played across his face, and he felt his heart jumping in his chest. It was working! The sirens were silent, fleeing. How could it be so simple? Kurian wondered. He wanted to laugh and shout with joy, and he poured that excitement into his song to the King.

When Mercia and Ham took their places in the line, Kurian waved them forward with his torch.

Searching

Entering the forest, a strong sense of danger fell upon Kurian. They were exposed again, outnumbered in their enemies' home. The torches threw shadows against the backdrop of the trees, creating the illusion of movement everywhere. It made him alert, but their plan was still working, and his excitement overcame the fear. He continued to sing with the others.

"Oh, call on the Rock, call on our Lord,
Who comes to our rescue with his mighty sword."

His eyes flitted from one motion or shape to another: the broad, dry leaves of a hawthorn waving in the breeze, the almost bare branches of a slender birch swaying in the higher wind coming from the sea.

"He shatters the sky with only a word,

Oh, call on the Rock, call on our Lord."

He could not see any sirens. Everyone stopped and listened when the song was over. Kurian couldn't hear anything.

He waited until the sirens started again to shout, "Captain Bacchus!"

A moment later, Louise called, "East." She had taken the wax from her ears, along with Mercia and Crispin, to hear calls for help.

They started up singing again. Their line swung toward the left, and they continued to walk and search slowly eastward.

They sang and wove through the trees and brush of the forest for another half mile, stopping only to listen and call for Cpt. Bacchus. Each time, the response was a little louder according to Louise and Crispin. Kurian also heard something nobody mentioned: a growing noise of footsteps and snapping branches behind them, and on their flanks. The hunters were silent, but gathering around them.

"I'm beginning to think you were right about a trap, Tobin," he said during a lull.

"Shall we close ranks?" Sage asked.

"Not yet," Kurian shouted as the sirens filled the silence.

Louise began their next song, drowning out the creatures again, but it was clear that their passage back to the cave was blocked. Kurian had the distinct impression they were being herded.

They continued another hundred yards, and suddenly the ash, beech, and chestnut trees vanished. Before them was an enormous, spreading oak in a clearing encircled by the smaller trees. The oak looked dead. Its branches were bare of leaves, and it glistened in the firelight. Kurian stepped forward and found it covered with damp, dark moss or fungus. He didn't know what it was, but he didn't want to touch it. The earthy scents of mushrooms, rotting wood, and dung filled the air around. Large branches sprawled, low and level, a few inches above his head. In the crooks, and atop the broader branches rested nests. The sirens screeched and moaned when Kurian approached the tree, despite the song his friends were still singing. The sight of the strange, diseased oak had caused them all to lose vigor.

"There must be dozens," Mercia said.

"I believe we've found their roost," said Sage. "Best not to linger." No sooner had he spoken than three of the sirens rushed out of the darkness with fury in their faces.

Kurian shouted, "Attack!"

Everyone whirled around, but their voices stopped in the surprise, except for Sage. He crooned strong and lofty above the clamor of the fight. He stopped the first two, while the other flanked Crispin and leapt at Kurian himself. All three of them tried to force their way to him. Sage and Louise killed another pair on their end, while Kurian ran forward to meet the challenge. With only Sage singing, more sirens appeared. Five came from Kurian's side, surrounding him. He swung his sword and his torch to defend himself, but neither connected. The sirens had become wary of the fire and the blade.

"Protect the King," Sage shouted, retreating from his new foe to bring their line into a circle. He cut down one siren from behind.

"Cover Mercia and Ham first," Kurian yelled back.

Tobin called over his shoulder, "They're after you, Kurian."

"We promised we'd get them home."

"Sing!" Sage reminded them.

"Call on the Rock, our Fortress, our Shield..."

The group sang out anew over the brawl. Immediately, the ferocity of the attack waned. The beasts cringed. Some tried to retreat. They were not allowed to return to the shadows.

"Quickly, past the tree," Kurian shouted. They ran around one side of the dead oak and back into the smaller trees of the forest. He heard the sirens pursuing, but they kept their distance.

They alternated now, some calling, some singing as they moved as quickly as possible under the canopy. The groans and wild shouts from the injured man grew louder. A shift in the breeze brought Kurian the pungent stench of rotting meat. After a few steps, it was so strong he coughed and gagged while singing.

"Bones," Crispin said beside him. Kurian looked where the boy pointed. Several long bones stood out white against the dark detritus of the forest floor.

"They're old," said Mercia, "bleached."

"Corpse," Sage called loudly.

Tobin jogged over to him and yelled back to everyone, "There's nothing left. I can't tell if it's him."

A shout rose from behind a downed tree a few yards away. Kurian ran and vaulted over the trunk. A cloud of flies erupted where he landed.

He turned to see Captain Bacchus propped between the branches. "Found him," he shouted.

Bacchus' hair was lighter than Kurian remembered, blond and matted around his shoulders. His beard had grown in light and patchy, and his face was grimy. His shirt was intact, but his pants lay tattered on his body. Only the right pant leg and boot remained intact. A large wound spread on his left calf, covered with flies.

The others came near, still singing, and Kurian held up a hand for them to stop. The sirens raised their wailing again as he leaned close to the captain. "Dilly," he said.

Bacchus raised his eyelids and groaned, "You again."

"He's exposed," Kurian said, "and I don't think he can walk."

"Only friends call me Dilly," Bacchus said.

The sirens got louder and leapt from the shadows. They made quick swipes before retreating into hiding. Kurian swung blindly at movement on his left and clubbed one with his torch. Sparks flew everywhere as the creature fell, and he jabbed his sword through its side.

"You are not a friend!" Bacchus shouted like a drunk.

"We're the only ones here to save you," Kurian said.

"You're hurting my loves," Bacchus wailed. He stared longingly at the dead siren and cried, "Oh, Simone. Beautiful even in death."

"Can you stand?" Kurian asked.

"No saving," Bacchus argued.

Mercia looked at Tobin. "He's got it worse than you, Loverboy." Then she coughed. "And it smells like he still wallows in his own filth."

"He's delirious," said Sage.

"He was a lunatic before," Mercia shrugged.

"Luna!" Bacchus shouted. "Have you murdered her, too?"

Sage climbed over the log and inspected Bacchus' leg. "The wound's infected." The sirens tried another lightning attack, jumping at anyone who wasn't singing.

"I don't think they like us playing with their food," Kurian said.

"If my pain or my death feeds them, how can I hold that against them?" Bacchus lamented with tears cutting down his filthy face.

"Get the sledge together quickly," Kurian ordered.

Weakening

Louise waved flies from her face. They swarmed around her and Mercia as they collected enough branches for the sledge. Tobin and Crispin found the sturdiest, straightest saplings they could and cut the extra sticks and twigs from them. Mercia and Louise gathered flexible switches to weave between the long poles. Ham and Kurian helped Sage to dress Bacchus' wound. The work should have gone quickly, but the sirens threatened them at every stage. Their singing was not as effective when they spread out. Louise could only carry a small bundle in one hand while she fended off the horrors jumping from the darkness with her torch.

She brought her third batch back to the group and lit a new torch. The failing one, she thrust into the moist ground, hoping it might give a little more protection to the men surrounding Bacchus. Then she thought better and asked Crispin to make a fire from the dead sticks he and Tobin cut.

"Good idea," said Crispin, beginning right away.

Louise waved for Tobin to follow her. "Help us gather more." She noticed Mercia making another face of displeasure and felt a mix of pity and annoyance. She understood what it was like for a girl to live in poverty in a coastal town. She had spent over a year in Downriver Town gathering information for the King. She had to deal with unwanted advances, even very aggressive ones. She knew the disgust and mistreatment of people who saw themselves as better than a poor girl. But Mercia used those experiences to color everything and everyone around her, except her brother. Of course, Louise also understood her being furious about the situation the siblings were in because of strangers. But Tobin was the least to blame, and the least likely ever to do what her glances accused him of.

While Mercia and Tobin sang, they collected branches, and Louise spoke, "Your dreams were true, and Kurian's." She spoke as much for Mercia to hear as for Tobin. Then she picked up the song.

"I'm amazed to see it," Tobin interjected between lines.

"I am every time," Louise said. She couldn't stop a grin from spreading wide across her face. "The King is truly with you both." A siren leapt over a small shrub. Louise instinctively lashed out with a branch. It slowed the attack, but the creature pushed her back, shredding the leaves and limbs before Tobin pierced its ribs with his sword.

"Let's get this done," he said, huffing, and sang again.

He was right. She saw each of them tiring. Their voices were not as strong after singing nonstop for over an hour. They were weary from fighting. And the sirens were more aggressive around the man they had claimed as their prize.

They got back to the others and Louise constructed the litter. She used smaller sticks between the long runners and lashed them together with the last of her cordage until they had a short ladder. Mercia was much better at knots than she was and finished it faster and stronger than Louise could have. Then they wove the slender limbs through the crossbars, singing the whole time.

Bacchus groaned. "Your dirge is more painful than my leg. No wonder my loves sound so tortured."

"You try singing half the night, and we'll see how your voice sounds," Mercia shouted back.

"It's not just your voices," he said. "It's the song. So dull."

"It keeps them from murdering us all," Kurian told him.

Louise spoke up, "Captain, would you be kind enough to let us save you without getting us killed?"

Bacchus quieted down for a moment but continued to groan and make comments under his breath the entire time they worked.

Tending

Kurian helped Sage to dress Bacchus' wounds, while the others constructed the litter to carry him. Heat radiated from the man's skin, and he was sweating despite the cold air of the autumn night. He screamed a couple of times and winced as Sage tried to clean the infected, inflamed gash on his left leg. Sage had stopped singing, and Kurian heard him praying quietly as he worked. Kurian sang louder to make up for Sage's silence, but the stench they had found earlier was also heavy around Bacchus. The sickening smell of infection and waste made Kurian gag with every few lines.

Kurian had seen infected cuts before, but never a knife wound with smaller holes—what looked like teeth marks—surrounding it. He expected puss, and oozing fluids, though not in such large amounts. What he didn't expect was the blackening flesh. Grit and dirt covered rigid, black skin, like dried meat at the edges of the wound.

Sage pointed to those portions and said, "That will not heal with normal methods."

"Why is the leg wet?" Kurian asked.

"That, I've never seen." Sage pointed. "These small punctures look like bites. It could be their saliva."

"That's right," Bacchus interjected, "they love me. I'm a tasty little morsel."

Kurian ignored him. Sage said, "It may have saved your life by slowing the infection."

"They couldn't bear to part with me," Bacchus crooned. "Ow!" he shouted as Sage went back to cleaning the leg.

Kurian cut a few strips from Bacchus' own shirt and tied them together to form a crude loincloth. He gave Ham some clean bandages from Louise's bag and motioned for him to tear it into strips for the injury. Ham understood immediately.

Kurian wondered what was going through Ham's mind. He couldn't imagine how Ham could handle all of this without fully understanding the circumstances. Mercia had told him something, but how much could she share with hand signs? Ham's face was stoic no matter what happened—except during a fight. There was fear in his expression when the sirens attacked, but his eyes were focused, determined. Though others might see the blank face as a sign of stupidity, Kurian expected that the story behind Ham's steely gaze was what kept Mercia going.

Bacchus complained about their singing again before bursting into song himself—the chorus of a bawdy tavern song. Kurian rolled up scraps of cloth and shoved it into the captain's mouth.

"Tobin," he called. "You don't happen to have any of that powder from the monastery, do you?"

"Unfortunately, not," said Tobin, looking up from the litter. "It would be nice to put him to sleep."

Escape

The moon was high over the beach, a helpful complement to their torches. The fire and the singing still held the sirens at bay, but they ventured closer to the light with every outburst from Bacchus. Like a lunatic, he removed the bandage Kurian had stuffed in his mouth to taunt them and call the creatures. Kurian left Sage and Ham to finish dressing the wounds and joined Crispin on guarding their flanks.

Sage declared the dressings finished at about the same time Louise and Mercia finished the litter. Tobin helped Sage to lift Bacchus onto the woven stretcher and tie him down for the ride.

Bacchus cried out once more, "Oh, Mara, Judith, my beautiful, horrible brides—save me from these altruists! These holy monks want to steal me from your healing kisses." After tying his arms, Tobin stuffed the cloth back in his mouth. A stream of muffled nonsense continued to pour from the captain.

Sage looked at the moon and sky and said, "Three hours after midnight. Ample time to return to the boat before sunrise."

Ham grabbed the poles at Bacchus' head before anyone asked. The others picked up their weapons and torches, then encircled the litter. From the front, Kurian gave the order, and they moved back into the timber. The moonlight waned under the canopy.

Immediately, sirens leapt from the darkness, a blur of claws and screaming faces met them. The surprise stopped Kurian from singing for a moment. He swung both torch and sword, cutting down three before he could look to the others. They were all fighting for their lives. The fury of the sirens became a frenzy.

One of them sped between him and Louise, going straight for Ham. Kurian cut her down mid-leap, but another tackled him from behind. His weapons went flying. Claws screeched on his armor. With no leverage to roll her off him, he craned his neck and saw a gaping maw of needle-like teeth about to sink into his neck.

Ham shoved his boot in her mouth, still holding the litter, and stepped over Kurian's head. It gave just enough time for Kurian to grapple the siren before she clawed Ham's leg open. Ham kept his foot in her mouth, pinning her skull to the ground, while Kurian rolled out and threw all his weight down and, breaking her neck.

Kurian retrieved his sword from beneath the creature but was already fighting again before he could recover his torch. He tried to sing, but the battle left his mouth dry.

Each siren they killed quickly became another, and they were being forced into a tighter ring around Bacchus and Ham. Kurian saw terror on each face. But Crispin, closest to the beach and the fire, was the only one not overwhelmed.

"Back to the beach," Kurian croaked with a thick tongue.

Crispin grabbed the other side of the litter, as if he had understood Kurian's every thought, and pulled Ham backward. Kurian turned and retreated slowly, fighting several more sirens before he was again between the fire and the ocean. The demons stopped their advance, pacing at the edge of the firelight. *Another standoff*, Kurian thought. *This island be damned.*

Sage grabbed his shoulder. "Why did we retreat?"

Kurian was out of breath, unable to answer.

"We were being overwhelmed," Tobin answered.

"I've faced worse odds before," Sage said, exasperated. "The King always brings us through."

"That may be," said Kurian, still huffing. "But I can't afford to lose anyone tonight. We don't have an army."

"What about your *thaumaturgy*?" Tobin asked Sage hopefully. "At the battle for Aposford, you called down lightning on Evasius' troops."

"I told you even tonight, that does not happen on command." Sage let go of Kurian's shoulder and turned to Tobin. "It is not my *thaumaturgy*, it is something in which I am allowed to take part. It is rarely the same. Not always dramatic. I only have faith that God will undoubtedly help in a manner he deems necessary."

Tobin's expression revealed he didn't like that answer. It was the first time Kurian could remember his best friend struggling to believe in divine assistance.

Kurian took a long drink, draining his small leather flask. "They're determined to stop us from taking Bacchus."

"Then let them have him," Mercia roared. Bacchus nodded his head and mumbled through his gag.

"No!" Kurian shouted. "It's why we came here. We'll be safe if we get back to the boats." He noticed sirens closing in from behind the log where they had tended the captain, and pointed. "They're trying to push us into the forest." Crispin ran forward and relit the pile of sticks and shavings left from constructing the litter. It slowed their advance.

"We have to use the beach," Kurian decided. "They have the advantage under the trees. Out here, we have the moon. The bay also protects our flank." He turned to Mercia. "Can you ask Ham if he can pull that thing on the sand?" She nodded, and after a moment signing to her brother, he nodded, too.

Kurian pointed to Tobin, "You're next if Ham needs help." After Tobin agreed, he added, "Let's try to get a little more fire to help us out." Then he batted the small campfire with his torch, sending sparks and embers toward the forest. Sirens scattered, and he rushed forward and touched his flame to the underbrush and driftwood.

The dry leaves lit and burned quickly. None of the larger kindling caught.

Sage laughed. "Good thought. But apparently, that's not the help we'll receive tonight."

Frustration welled up in Kurian and he yelled into the dark under the trees. The sirens shrieked in return. Their song resounded with new strength and he staggered with confusion and dizziness.

Sage pulled him back from the timberline. "Rage won't help right now."

Kurian shrugged off Sage's hand. "Down the beach," he said.

He suddenly feared not all of them would return, but he kept singing. It was the only thing left preventing a full attack. The hope he'd had when he first witnessed Louise's voice silence the Song and push back the monsters was waning. His throat was dry, and his voice was cracking from the strain of singing for hours. The others had also lost their fervor.

Beach

They trudged down the beach across loose stones and coarse wet sand, staying close to the water. Kurian felt like his voice barely rose above the lapping tide. The sirens followed near the tree line. Sometimes they disappeared, and only the rustling shrubs or snapping twigs signaled their presence. Ham struggled to drag the litter on the beach. It frequently dug deeply or snagged on buried rocks. The small, smooth pebbles made it hard to control in areas where the beach sloped steeply.

Kurian listened to Ham's struggle for a tenth of a mile before he fell back and picked up the other side of the sledge. Tobin took his place in the lead with both their torches. Kurian had to be more cautious about his footing, but the change helped them move faster. He continued to croak out the song, and his eyes welled up with the exhaustion and fear. He wanted to believe as Sage did, but the voice inside that had led him since his meeting with the King was silent. This night so full of terror made him doubt they would succeed. The only hope left within him was that they were nearly halfway to the boats.

"Stop," Tobin called.

Kurian looked up and saw sirens pouring out of the forest fifty yards ahead. He counted eighteen in the moonlight as they paced the beach, blocking the way.

"Keep singing," Sage said. "Renew your enthusiasm." His voice was raspy, too.

Kurian coughed. "I'm having trouble getting out anything." He lowered the poles of the litter and drew his sword again.

"We all are," Louise agreed. Her voice came back flat and tired, though still with more life than Kurian's own.

"Sage," Kurian said. "I've been praying, and I hear nothing. I don't know what to do. What about you?"

"He has been silent in my spirit as well," Sage replied. "But the King has already given us a weapon against them."

"A weapon we won't have much longer," said Mercia. Her singing had degraded to a chant.

"Do they mean to stop us or drive us into the forest?" Sage wondered aloud. "If we fortify our hearts and voices to push forward, they will retreat."

"Unless they intend to wait us out," Tobin offered. "They recognize our weakness."

At that moment, a smaller group of sirens emerged from the timber at their rear, cutting off escape.

"We could use something dramatic now, Sage," Crispin said, voice cracking.

Mercia stepped before Ham and signed with him briefly. She tapped her head, then opened her mouth and pushed her open hand forward from it and finally cupped his face in her hands and mouthed "Mama." He looked confused before he nodded.

In a low, awkward tone, Ham sang a lullaby. Kurian recognized it deep within his memory.

"I saw a fair maiden, sitting and sing,
She lulled a little child a sweet lording:
'Lullay, mine liking, my dear son, mine sweeting,
Lullay, my dear heart, mine own dear darling.'"

"Now that is a lay I know," Sage smiled. He joined in quietly, his voice as weak as Kurian felt.

The rest of them stopped singing for a moment to listen and drink whatever they had left. The group of sirens approached slowly from behind, silent on the beach.

Ham's music by itself seemed to make them cautious. But whether because it was quiet, or because he could not hold the melody clearly, it did not push them back in the same way.

"They're coming," Crispin said. He began the other songs again. He stopped after a few bars and said, "I can't sing with a different song going. The words get mixed up."

Mercia motioned to Ham. He raised his voice, but the melody only suffered more.

"How can he sing?" Louise asked.

Mercia snapped back, "Because he wasn't always deaf."

The sirens advanced, closing the gap from behind, while the ones ahead paced in a line. Tobin was the first to say out loud what Kurian was thinking: "They're using strategy."

"Many predators do," observed Sage. "We must be wiser."

"What do we do?" Mercia asked, more fearful than before.

Kurian felt a surge of determination to overcome the fear that plagued him. It wasn't the King speaking in his spirit, but it reminded him of the confidence and surety he had known before they faced Evasius. "We counter," he said, "stop them from boxing us in."

All eyes were suddenly on him. He saw the mix of fear and expectation he had seen in the people of Aposford before the battle. This was the look of people wanting leadership and hope. Sage was the only one who looked pleased and self-assured in response, as if he were choosing to follow willingly. The others looked like a craving had just been satisfied.

"Tobin," he said, "I count eight coming in behind. Can you handle them with me?" He waited for a nod. "We attack fast, try to surprise them. The rest of you stand your ground and sing if you can." Kurian pulled his shield from his back. Tobin staked the torches in the gravel and readied his own weapons.

The sirens continued their silent progress as if nothing had changed. With only Ham singing, the siren song quietly emerged from the larger group, but the ones approaching were quiet. Kurian steeled his will against the sound and whispered, "Hold," to Tobin. The sirens crept closer, within fifty feet. A few more steps and they would be close enough to leap on him. He counted their strides in his head. *One. Two. Three. Four.*

"Now," he whispered. He and Tobin dashed forward together. They closed the gap with such speed that their enemies had little chance to react. They startled and jumped like stray cats being charged by a dog. In unison, Kurian and Tobin dropped their first foes. One leapt over Kurian's head, almost to Crispin. Kurian focused on the next. The third finally fought back. It lashed out with its claws and dodged Kurian's sword. Another pounced but ricocheted off his shield before Tobin pierced it from behind. Kurian lunged at the fighter, but only wounded it as it spun and ran into the woods. It was the only one he remembered having blond hair, and he watched as she fled into the forest. The golden strands shone brightly in the moonlight and bounced with her steps, except for a growing dark spot where the hair clung to her back.

"Kurian!" Tobin shouted.

He turned and saw the siren who had leapt over him dead at Crispin's feet. He heard Bacchus roaring through his gag and straining at his bonds. The sirens blocking the beach ahead moved forward. But from the trees directly across from his friends, another crowd rushed in to attack. Some broke off and ran toward Kurian and Tobin. "They'll split us," said Tobin, taking off at a sprint.

Kurian mustered all he could from his lungs and belted out a song through his raspy throat.

"O Caprics, my brothers, you've nothing to fear;
Our God who stands o'er us will fill you with cheer."

He knew none of the others would know it, but when he caught up with Tobin, he saw a smile as his best friend fought.

Together, they clashed with the monsters in the moonlight and sang the song from their childhood. Kurian killed a siren with almost every blow, but there was always another. They had moved quickly enough that they soon reached the others and joined in with their song. But the creatures fought viciously. Kurian felt their desperation to stop the invaders from escaping with their prize. He pushed his muscles through the strain, alternately killing the sirens, protecting his friends, or being saved in return.

A siren fell wounded at his feet and reached up with a gaping mouth. She bit down on his thigh before he could counter. Needle-teeth sank into his hamstrings. He yelled out and drove his sword through her neck. In a lull, he saw Crispin receive a scratch on his face. Louise dropped when a siren landed on top of her and gouged a talon into her shoulder. Sage kicked the beast off her. Mercia delivered the killing blow with Ham's knife. He saw them all weakening. It felt like their final stand.

Suddenly, the two he faced staggered back as if battered by an invisible foe. He slew one, and the other retreated, clambering up the beach. The rest pulled back, too, without warning, but they held their ground at the tree line. Only a few remained from the ambush.

"What happened?" Louise asked through heaving breaths. She glanced down at her shoulder and grimaced.

"I don't know," Kurian wheezed. "But I...can't sing." The last two words were barely a whisper. His voice was gone.

Crispin pointed to himself and nodded but didn't speak. Blood trickled down his jaw from his cheek.

"You don't have to," Sage smiled. "Our help has come."

Kurian waited for him to say more, but Sage's smile only broadened as he tapped his ear.

The sharp trill of a blackbird cut into the night. It broke through the wax and bandages as sunbeams through a fog.

At the sound, the sirens shivered and shook their heads like someone pestered by a gnat.

"I don't understand," Tobin said.

Bacchus finally spit out the rag and shouted, "Stop this! They hate the damned songbirds, you murderers."

"Shut it!" Mercia ordered, stuffing the gag back in his mouth.

The blackbird let out its song again. A second answered.

"He's right," said Sage. "When we could no longer sing, God sent his birds to help us."

"Nonsense," Mercia challenged, "blackbirds sing hours before dawn all the time."

"But not always when it will save our lives. How did they and we come to be at this precise moment and place?" Sage asked.

"Because birds sing in trees," Mercia sneered, and waved at the forest. "It's only a coincidence they upset the sirens."

As soon as she spoke, the two birdsongs became a multitude, their songs calling back and forth, overlapping. More joined every second, the volume increasing until the birdsong covered the island like a blanket of sound. The blackbirds tweeted and chirped in an unending, unbroken symphony. Kurian thought there must have been thousands in the trees to make such a noise. The sirens either ran down the beach or fell to the ground and clawed the air.

Sage shrugged his shoulders and said to Mercia, "If the lady insists."

Final

Sage rushed toward the trees with no warning. Everyone else watched in surprise as he attacked the sirens that had fallen on the ground. Some swiped at his feet, others rose to meet him, but only for a moment. None of them could resist the distraction of the new song with enough willpower to defend against him. No sounds of the conflict reached Kurian over the chorus of blackbirds. It seemed as if they trilled for the battle.

Kurian was surprised to see the man normally so gentle breaking out in violence against creatures that were practically defenseless. He scanned the faces of the others. Mercia looked both shocked and gratified. Louise's face wrinkled in uncertainty. Tobin had fallen to his knees in prayer and missed most of the action. Crispin had an exhausted look of relief and admiration. Ham was the only one who charged after Sage and joined the slaughter.

Together, they raced down the beach after the sirens who had fled. Mercia followed her brother. Tobin pursued the rest when his eyes opened. Kurian cleaned his sword and sheathed it, strapped his shield to his back, and tapped Crispin on the shoulder. When the boy looked at him, he pointed to Bacchus' feet, then picked up the head of the litter.

"We need to keep up," he croaked, but all that he could hear from himself was, "eep up."

Louise nodded and grabbed two torches. Kurian tugged on the poles, and they began a hurried march toward the boat. With the weight of Bacchus and the rocky shore, they didn't move quickly enough. The others pushed forward through the broken barricade of sirens, gaining ground and leaving Kurian's group behind.

Bacchus cried out and occasionally thrashed, throwing his weight to the side and causing Kurian or Crispin to stumble.

"Stop that," Crispin chided.

Louise even tried to calm him, but the captain was inconsolable in his grief for the sirens.

When Crispin nearly fell from one of Bacchus' lunges, Louise took his place.

Tobin broke from the fighting and raced back. "I'm sorry I left," he said, panting. "When I saw Sage's fervor, I felt compelled to fight. And when I saw Mercia running, I thought she might need protection." Kurian only nodded. His voice was useless.

"It's incredible," Tobin said. "We've routed them, and we have a clear path to the boats." Tobin paused. "What's wrong?"

Kurian tossed his head forward, trying to indicate for Tobin to lead the way. Tobin's elation vanished. His eyes dropped and he nodded curtly, then took the lead.

Crispin jogged up to Tobin's side. "That was more incredible than when you saved me and threw me through the smoke."

"I got carried away," Tobin said. "I shouldn't have abandoned you all."

"I meant the birds," Crispin choked out.

"Look," said Louise.

Kurian saw Sage, Ham, and Mercia just as they entered the trees some distance ahead. He grunted.

"What are they doing?" asked Crispin.

Tobin answered, "I think they're pursuing the sirens. We were in something of a frenzy there."

Kurian tried to clear his throat to speak, but nothing came out. Tobin looked at him, and he nodded his head toward the others, and then toward the boats.

"I think he wants you to go get them," Louise said.

"I know," said Tobin before jogging off after them.

Crispin turned. "Can I go, too?"

"No, Cris," Louise said. "We might still need protection here."

Her words proved true a few moments later when they reached the carnage that had been the barricade on the beach. Bodies littered the ground between the tide and the trees, but not all the sirens were dead. One lunged at Crispin, despite severe injuries, startling him. He finished it instantly, then was on guard against anything else that might move on the ground.

With Louise carrying Bacchus' feet, they moved faster and arrived at the cove in half an hour. As they walked, the birdsong quieted down to a normal level, a few birds singing back and forth. Robins and wrens soon joined the blackbirds, though they never reached the cacophony of their first crescendo. If not for the terror of the night, Kurian realized it would be a beautiful, peaceful place. He barely glimpsed the boats at anchor. The moon hovered over them, reflected in the calm water. A breeze pushed Bacchus' stench away from him and brought the damp, earthy smell of fall.

He scanned the beach and saw nothing else. *Where are they,* he wondered just before Crispin and Louise said the same.

Branches cracked in the woods, mingled with intermittent sounds of struggle; claws against steel, metal against wood, keening, and roaring. After the birds had quieted to a normal level, the horrible, painful song of the sirens had returned. It was faint, but Kurian still felt it in his gut.

Why didn't they come straight away? There was no escape without someone to retrieve the boats.

They set Bacchus down a few feet above the tide. He had finally fallen asleep. The torches Crispin carried were weakening. Kurian grabbed some loose driftwood and built a fire to keep all of them warm. The sounds from the forest continued, drawing nearer, occasionally fading to silence for a few moments before breaking out again. Birds sang in the trees as if it were a typical predawn morning for them. In one lull, Kurian even heard an early cock-crow coming over the water from Whalesand. They waited an hour before hearing a whistle from the forest. Louise put her fingers in her mouth and let out a piercing reply.

The fighting started again, and a few moments later, three sirens burst from the woods. Kurian thought they were attacking until he saw his friends appear behind them. The creatures fled blindly. Kurian, Louise, and Crispin cut them down more to avoid them running over Bacchus than in defense. The others stepped forward, breathless and filthy. Ham dripped with dark, glistening blood. Mercia and Sage had small limbs clinging to them. She laughed quietly with a wild look in her eyes. Blood stained her light tunic all the way up the sleeves and across the front. Ham walked straight into the water and swam for the boats.

"They wouldn't come until the fight was over," Tobin huffed. Kurian couldn't say anything, but he shared a long stare with Sage, trying to find an answer for the sudden recklessness.

Louise asked what he was thinking. "Why did you leave us?"

Sage continued looking at Kurian, not speaking until his breathing had slowed. "Your pardon if I sinned. I saw that the help we prayed for had arrived and that the battle was ours."

"Did you kill all of them?" she asked.

"I pray we did," Sage answered her directly.

She objected, "They were nearly defenseless."

Kurian wished he could speak, wished he could ask the questions and find the answers himself, but Louise expressed what was on his mind. He understood the heat of the battle and getting carried away with a fight, but they had not come to slaughter creatures who were no threat.

"For how long?" Sage asked. "Do not be fooled by their re-semblance to women. These were beasts of evil. Their only purpose in the world is destruction and death. How many innocent lives have they already taken?"

"Only *one* I know of," Mercia said bitterly.

Sage continued as if he hadn't heard. "How many lives would they take if we had spared the lot? How long before they were back to their full strength and threatened every passing ship?"

"What if they ever found a way off the island?" Tobin added.

"I'm not comfortable with slaughter," Louise said. "I don't think the King would want that."

Mercia stepped forward and glared up at her, inches away. "Have you ever seen your king fight monsters? That's what these were. If you don't know that, you're closing your own eyes."

Through their bickering, Kurian still heard the siren song, faint in its lament. While they argued, he saw one emerge from the trees where the last fighting had occurred. Even though it stumbled, it moved with smooth, seductive grace as it bent down to touch each of its fallen sisters. When it had finished, it stood watching from a distance. He recognized it as the blonde one he had wounded. Its song was so faint, it almost felt like a tune barely remembered, a dirge he had heard in infancy.

Sage broke from the argument and strode toward the siren. Kurian tried to call out to stop him, but his voice wouldn't carry.

Sage's body blocked Kurian's view of the encounter, but as he turned to walk back, the Song faded slowly into silence. One songbird sang out. Then the only sound was the soft whisper of the tide.

Mercia watched the last siren fall and sobbed. Her legs buckled and she dropped to the ground, crying and moaning on her hands and knees.

Ham returned dripping from the sea, handed the line for the boats to Kurian and kneeled beside his sister. When he touched her back, she looked up.

Through her sobs, she smiled and said, "Ham. We did it. He can rest now."

Kurian shared a look with Louise, but nobody interrupted them.

Return

Kurian tapped Tobin on the shoulder and pointed toward the boats.

"We did it," Tobin said. "Let's get back." Tobin cupped a grimy, gritty hand aside Kurian's head. Kurian saw the relief in his eyes as he whispered, "And everyone's safe."

Kurian nodded before glancing at Bacchus.

Tobin and Sage lifted the captain into one boat. Louise and Crispin climbed aboard before Kurian pushed them off the sand and clambered in beside Crispin. The others boarded the second boat. Sage was the last on the beach. Kurian picked up his oar and watched as the ancient monk paused and listened, scanning the beach and the edge of the forest. The young king didn't know whether the old warrior was praying or looking for threats, but it led him to pray himself. He thanked God and the King for their success, and he asked for the strength and wisdom to handle the dangerous monk on the shore, the mysterious man of God who threw lightning at his enemies and destroyed everything he regarded as evil. Sage turned, saw Kurian watching, and bowed to the young man he accepted as king before leaping deftly into the stern of his boat. Kurian didn't trust he could lead such a wild man. He wondered: *will Sage be a help or a hindrance as we try to restore the kingdom?*

Crispin spoke.

"What?" Kurian asked without sound, then realized he still had wax in his ears.

He paused rowing to pull off the bandage and dig out the wax. It was like emerging from a dream. He heard the water lapping on the boat, and the wood creaking. He listened to the birds singing on the island, and gulls beginning to cry from the docks in Whalesand. Every sound was clear again, and it brought Kurian back to the moment.

"Do you think he'll make it?" Crispin asked, looking at Bacchus.

Louise answered, "I don't think the King would have had us save him only to let him die on the mainland." Her voice was low and rough. She sounded much older.

Crispin nodded, and they continued to row in silence.

The beach and the cove retreated from their vision and became just another part of the island as the stars faded into lightness on the eastern horizon. Kurian's body ached. The bite in his thigh stung as it rubbed the wooden seat. All he wanted was sleep. The methodical rhythm of rowing dulled his mind, and he closed his eyes as he pulled the boat across the bay with Crispin.

A long groan made him open his eyes. Bacchus stared up at him from the bottom of the boat. He yawned, then winced. Recognition finally filled his face.

"Young Kurian," Bacchus said with a small smile. "Did we make it past the sirens?"

Louise leaned over her knees to show her face. "*We* did."

Bacchus tried to move. "Why am I bound?"

"Rest now," Louise whispered. "We'll tell you everything later."

"I'd rather not," Bacchus said. His gaze lost focus and he added, "It's as if I've just woken from the most seductively terrifying dream."

He leered at her. "It was delicious." Her eyes welled up, and she turned away to wipe her cheek.

When he saw her reaction, his facade faded. "I didn't want it to be real," he said flatly. "I feel like they have dragged me over a reef."

Bacchus shifted his gaze and stared at Kurian a long time. Finally, he spoke: "I told you I could trust your scruples."

Kurian opened his mouth to try speaking, then decided against it. He nodded once, then closed his eyes again and pulled on the oar.

Restore

As soon as they reached Whalesand, Kurian and Sage picked up the sleeping Bacchus and carried him to his ship, the Osprey. The others followed. One of the dark-haired and bearded men was leaning over the railing of the ship. When he saw them coming, he called over his shoulder, "Captain Darling."

Cpt. Darling appeared at his side, and his eyes slowly grew wide as he recognized the filthy and tattered group approaching on the dock. He walked down the gangway and strode toward Kurian, nearly bumping him in the chest. "What in all the seas happened to you?" he asked. A crowd of sailors joined the first one at the railing to watch.

Kurian looked at him with weary eyes. "Bacchus is alive," he wheezed.

Darling leaned and peered over Kurian's shoulder before grunting, "Barely."

"Barely is still alive," said Louise, "and you're the only people in Whalesand who care enough to keep him that way."

"I didn't ask for your opinion, girl," Bacchus said. "You always let her speak for you?" he asked Kurian.

"When she's right," Kurian said, then coughed uncontrollably.

Darling faced out toward the water and the blue horizon layered with purple and pink clouds in the early light. A breeze pushed at his thick beard. He remained silent long after Kurian's coughing fit. Finally, he slapped his bald head. "We'll take him," he nodded. "Men would mutiny if I refused. We'll make him comfortable as we can. Bury him at sea when he's gone."

Kurian shook his head, then gestured to the boat on the beach they had bought from Cpt. Darling. "Boat. Money. Yours."

"It should be enough for a physician," Tobin said hoarsely. Kurian was glad for his best friend to interpret his intent.

Darling again sought his counsel in the sea.

Finally, he sighed. "Could use my partner. Made more silver with him for less work." The crowd of sailors on the Osprey cheered and descended the gangplank. They took the stretcher from Kurian and Sage and pranced their beloved captain back onto the ship. Once aboard, they started a jolly shanty and capered across the deck.

As Kurian walked away, Darling asked, "How did ye do it?"

Mercia strode forward with a terrifying grin of satisfaction. Matted hair covered one eye like a veil.

"We killed them all," she growled. She tried to brush the hair off her face, but the dried blood kept it in place.

"But how?"

"You always knew we were different," was all she said.

Darling remained stoic. Then he waved a hand dismissively and climbed back onto his ship.

As they walked off the dock, Louise asked Mercia if she might stay with them, instead of at the inn. When Mercia hesitated, Louise added, "Just enough to clean up and rest before we return to the plain."

Mercia consulted with her brother. "You may," she told Louise. "When you leave, we're coming with you."

Kurian stopped walking. "Why?" he fought to ask.

"After what we saw last night?" Mercia fumbled her words, struggling to grasp the night before. Her abusive confidence fell away. "Ham wants to go with you. He's curious. And I go where Ham goes."

"It will be dangerous," Sage said. Kurian noticed what seemed a trained look of empathy as he counseled the girl, like something his teachers had tried to develop in him and his friends.

"More dangerous than spending a night fighting monsters?"

Sage nodded. "We know not what stands before us. King Kurian was victorious and routed Evasius, but he only retreated to his stronghold. I see an abundance of battle and hardship in our future. The Lord of Pallingham will not cease devising evil while he breathes."

Mercia spent a moment signing to her brother. He clenched his jaw and nodded firmly.

"Ham is certain," she said. "If he goes, I have nothing here but bad memories."

Louise and Tobin looked at Kurian. He shrugged his shoulders and threw her a cockeyed smile. A friendly grin spread across Louise's face. She seemed to enjoy speaking for him. She looked at the siblings and said, "You are more than welcome in the King's camp."

"That's done," said Tobin. "Now might we find a bed?"

Get the latest on the next book in the King of The Caves series.

Sign up for my free newsletter at:
brandonwilborn.com

You'll also find other stories from Brandon M. Wilborn, and get reviews and suggestions for other books you might enjoy.

Author's Note

First, thank you for reading this book. I hope that you enjoyed it, and even more, I hope that it lingers and makes you think about the nature of temptation and how we deal with it. Please take the time to review it on your favorite store by going to **books2read.com/SirenSilence**, because it helps other readers find books they'll enjoy.

If this is your first experience with Kurian, you may feel as if you've missed a lot. You did.

This is just a novella that follows *The Treasure of Capric*, book one in *The King of the Caves*. You can find it at your favorite retailer through this link: **books2read.com/TreasureofCapric**

Shortly after finishing that book, I knew that I would tell the story of what happened to Cpt. Bacchus after he leapt into the sea toward the sirens, and that story is now complete.

If you've read both stories, I hope it will please you to hear that book Two of *The King of the Caves* has a rough course plotted and is working its way onto paper now. I pray that it will be complete in 2019. Please be patient with me to discover what happens with Kurian and the King. Or if you'd like to nudge me to hurry up, you can email me at brandon@brandonwilborn.com

No spoilers will be provided.

Blessings,
Brandon M Wilborn

Acknowledgements

My first thanks always must go to my wife. These books would not exist without her support. Her words of wisdom and truth continue to inspire and encourage me.

Secondly, I must thank my editor, Tracy Cartwright. While she edits for a living, she went the extra mile to read my first book a second time so as not to miss any details while editing this novella. I continue to be impressed with my cover designer, Darko Tomic. Included at this level, I must thank Veronika Wunderer, who made my sketch of Pallingham respectable.

Finally, I offer thanks to my initial readers. My brother Dennis continues to be one of my most involved supporters. His insights pushed me to write the final scene. Those who read the full manuscript and helped at launch time include Adrienne S., Bomi W., Iesha D., Kendra L., Melanie M., and Michele W. Your support means the world to me. Thank you.

ABOUT THE AUTHOR

Brandon Wilborn is a man with too many interests, and one great love. No, three great loves. Well, five. So far.

But for the purposes here, he has one great love, and that is science fiction and fantasy. (Speculative fiction, if you insist on the singular.) He first fell in love with the fantastical and mythical while playing *The Legend of Zelda* and watching an old cartoon of *The Hobbit* when he was four years old. That eventually led him to dream of writing.

He has now authored *The Treasure of Capric*, his first novel and book one of *The King of the Caves* series, along with a follow-up novella, *Siren Silence: The Fate of Captain Bacchus.*

His love of science fiction and fantasy, along with an education in English and Theological Studies, inspired him to create stories that are full of epic adventure while grappling with deeper questions of life, faith, and our role in the drama of good and evil.

After a wandering youth in a Navy family, growing up primarily in Hawaii, and then wandering a bit more, he has now found a happy home with three of his great loves in Idaho. Find more of his stories and the latest release information for book two of *The King of the Caves* at BrandonWilborn.com